"This isn't happening," she whispered.

"Something sure as hell is," he muttered, sounding angry and lost too all of a sudden. "I should have stood my ground and stayed in London."

"You could always just go."

"No, it's too late now. The damage is done." His eyes devoured hers, and she thought he stared straight into her soul, which had always belonged only to him. "I've seen you. I've touched you. And I'm curious...about a lot of things."

She didn't understand the stillness that possessed her, held her and him. Was she in a trance? Was he? Clasped tightly against his tall, muscular body, his heat flooding her, she could barely think, barely breathe.

"I'm going to hate you for this," she whispered, and then she kissed him.

Dear Reader,

While I grew up in a city in south Texas, the rest of my family lived in a small Texas ranching town near the Panhandle. One of the highlights of my summers back then was visiting my cousins up north and riding their horse, Gypsy, bareback...all day long. Maybe Gypsy didn't enjoy this as much as we did because she regularly bucked us off.

Stories about independent women who love horses became a part of me early on. I've always liked reunion romances too. So, why not a reunion romance about a horse woman and the cowboy who left her behind to become a billionaire in London?

Six years later, when Luke returns home, Caitlyn is a widow with a son. Her ranch is heavily mortgaged and she is in danger of losing her horses.

Luke is the last man Caitlyn wants to have anything to do with. When Luke learns her son is his, he offers to help her...for a price. Of course, the price they will both have to pay for their new life together is love.

Enjoy,

Ann Major

P.S. Visit me at www.annmajor.com!

Marriage at the Cowboy's Command

ANN MAJOR

MILLS & BOON®

First published in Great Britain 2012
by Mills & Boon, an imprint of Harlequin (UK) Limited.
Large Print edition 2012
Harlequin (UK) Limited,
Eton House, 18-24 Paradise Road,
Richmond, Surrey TW9 1SR

© Ann Major 2011

ISBN: 978 0 263 22966 0

Harlequin (UK) policy is to use papers that are natural, renewable and recyclable products and made from wood grown in sustainable forests. The logging and manufacturing process conform to the legal environmental regulations of the country of origin.

Printed and bound in Great Britain
by CPI Antony Rowe, Chippenham, Wiltshire

ANN MAJOR

lives in Texas with her husband of many years and is the mother of three grown children. She has a master's degree from Texas A&M at Kingsville, Texas, and is a former English teacher. She is a founding board member of the Romance Writers of America and a frequent speaker at writers' groups.

Ann loves to write; she considers her ability to do so a gift. Her hobbies include hiking in the mountains, sailing, ocean kayaking, traveling and playing the piano. But most of all she enjoys her family. Visit her website at www.annmajor.com

This book is dedicated to
Stacy Boyd and Shana Smith and
the Desire team. Their names do
not appear on the cover, but they
worked very hard to improve this
story, and I am deeply in their debt.

<u>One</u>

Desperation mounting, Caitlyn Wakefield stared at her accounting ledgers. There was no way she could make her next mortgage payment to Sheik Hassan Bin Najjar. No way.

So, what would she say to Hassan's mysterious honorary son, Raffi Bin Najjar, when he showed up today to check on her operation?

She had no clue.

She'd gone over the books numerous times, hoping she'd figure out how to make her next payment and get her ranch on a viable financial footing, but all she saw were too many fixed expenses without enough income.

Even if she asked Hassan for more time, which she believed he would give her, she needed to make some serious and painful adjustments or she'd just be deeper in debt down the line. She couldn't expect Hassan to bankroll her forever.

The awful numbers began to blur and her head to pound.

She hated disappointing Hassan. She wanted to make him proud of her. But the sales she'd counted on hadn't materialized. And she was again on the verge of losing her ranch, just as she'd been six months ago when Hassan had helped her by buying her mortgage.

It was nothing short of a miracle that Hassan, one of the world's richest sheiks, had become her friend, benefactor and banker. The fact that he was wealthy and she was not and that he spent most of his time in the Middle East and Europe while she lived in Texas would have been more than enough to keep them from ever knowing one another but for their mutual passion for Thoroughbreds.

They'd met by chance at the September yearling sales in Keeneland, Virginia, more than a year ago. Her timely advice had saved Hassan from buying an overpriced animal that had gone lame a mere four months later during a race, causing a jockey's death. The animal had been destroyed. The sheik had written her a note, thanking her, saying he would have hated being involved in a tragedy of that magnitude.

Then, six months ago, he'd phoned her again when Sahara, one of his most promising Thoroughbreds, developed a problem with starting gates. Caitlyn had been stunned by the sheik's offer to come to his stables in Deauville to work with the animal—for three times her normal fee.

It was just after her success with Sahara that he'd gotten to the bottom of her financial distress over a dinner they'd shared. Soon after, he bought her note from the bank.

Considering how much Hassan had done for her, she hated disappointing him. What could she say to his honorary son that would reassure Hassan?

Frustrated, she slammed the books shut. Only when her gaze fell to the small snapshot of her son, Daniel, riding bareback did her expression soften.

He'd been forbidden to ride the horse by himself, of course. Smiling, she picked up the picture and stared at his slim, dark likeness. Even when he was driving her crazy by being too curious or foolhardy, he filled her long days with joy. He was five, all boy and way too big for his britches a lot of the time, but she remembered how proud she'd been of him at Keeneland last year. Hassan, too, had been impressed with Daniel. So much so that he'd told her about his only biological son, Kalil, whom he'd nearly lost to a kidnapping in Paris a few years earlier.

"That's when I made Raffi, the man who rescued Kalil, my honorary son," Hassan had said.

She had smiled politely, her mind on the animals in the various pens and on Daniel, who'd been darting about under their feet.

"Your son reminds me of Raffi. So much energy. Once that energy is harnessed, he will be formidable."

"Really?" she'd replied, not paying much attention to Hassan's remark.

"Yes, even Daniel's eyes resemble Raffi's. They are the same shade of green. It's an unusual color in my part of the world."

"In ours, too," she'd said absently. "His father had green eyes."

They'd talked more, about Texas and her ranch. He'd asked for a card.

"Raffi once lived in Texas…in your vicinity, I believe." Hassan's gaze, more intent than before, had been on Daniel.

Ever since that first meeting at Keeneland, in all his calls and notes, Hassan always asked about Daniel. His grandfatherly interest in her son had become one of the chief reasons she liked the sheik so much.

Setting down Daniel's picture, she tried to refocus on the problem at hand. She hated that she could think of nothing that would turn Wild Horse Ranch around. Not that she wasn't used to being broke. When she was a child, her parents had constantly worried about bills and creditors. Never would she forget the day her father had told her and her mother that he'd lost their ranch. When they'd been forced to move into town and lease land for their ranching operation, she'd felt shattered. Nearly as shattered as she'd be if she couldn't win Raffi Bin Najjar's sympathy.

Chewing a fingernail, she went to the window and stared out at the sea of brown grasses. The early December air had been cool and crisp an hour before dawn, when she'd arisen. Her only indulgence before coming to her office was a single cup of strong black coffee.

To give me strength, she thought as she circled the cold cup with her fingertips.

What could she say to a stranger who probably knew little about ranching, even if he'd spent time in Texas? How could he—a wealthy, sophisticated man, who lived in London—possibly appreciate the calamity the worst drought in decades had wrought on her ranch and horse farm? How could a bachelor sympathize when she told him she'd been distracted and unfocused after her husband's death, when she'd had her grief, his work and hers and her son to take care of? How could a billionaire understand the effect of an entire country mired in recession? Everybody wanted to sell their horses, not buy hers.

Her income had diminished while her expenses had continued to mount. Business was picking up. But not quickly enough.

Swigging back the last of her cold coffee, she tried not to think about being the second Cooper to lose the ranch despite all her sacrifices to save it. The biggest sacrifice being her marriage to Robert, when she'd found herself pregnant and alone nearly six years ago. Not wanting to remember what had led to her wedding day, she fled to the stalls to feed her beloved horses.

Sensing her anxiety from the rapid ring of her boot heels on the concrete floor of the barn, Angel and the other horses swung their necks around and watched her with their concerned brown eyes. Their tails lifted and swished expectantly while the barn cats swirled at her feet.

Odd, the profound comfort she always felt when alone in the barn with these huge animals. Their soulful silence as she stroked them brought her peace during times of stress.

Angel nuzzled Caitlyn's hand with her whiskery muzzle, searching for a treat. "Robert was a bad manager," Caitlyn whispered to the horse, "and I'm no better. I spend too much money on all of you, my precious darlings." Angel nickered softly as if she understood. "I need a miracle, and soon."

Angel snorted.

"Well, it's possible! Hassan says his son is a billionaire, that there's nothing he can't fix. Raffi made his fortune in a mere five years, you see, by buying distressed companies."

Perhaps she could convince him that a distressed ranch wasn't that different from a company in trouble. She felt a faint twinge of hope as she remembered what Hassan had said when he'd shamelessly bragged about his son.

In a recent phone conversation, when she'd complained of her escalating expenses, Hassan had told her she was a woman of talent who shouldn't have to worry about money.

"I will send my son to devise a plan to put you on sound footing. He will know just what to do once he takes a look at your operation. He is a brilliant businessman."

She'd been scheduled to meet this brilliant businessman six months ago, when the sheik had flown her to Deauville to work with Sahara. Hassan had told her that Raffi would dine with them, but his son had been unexpectedly called away on business.

To prepare for their meeting today, she'd researched Raffi, but there hadn't been many articles about him or a single good photograph. Most of the stories rehashed the event that had brought Hassan and Raffi together, a tale she'd heard from Hassan.

Five years earlier, after Raffi had single-handedly confronted three terrorists to rescue Kalil, Hassan had hired him. Raffi advanced rapidly and, with the sheik's money behind him, had soon branched out on his own. The sheik had sealed their bond by making Raffi his honorary son. During their shared dinner in Deauville, Hassan had confided that he would like to see Raffi settle down and raise a family.

From what she'd gleaned on the internet about the younger Mr. Bin Najjar's private life, he went through women the way some men ran through cigars. But a woman like her—a horse trainer who wore old jeans and rarely bothered with makeup—wouldn't interest him.

"What do you think, Angel? Should I go the extra mile and put on lipstick?"

Angel whinnied enthusiastically, probably because Caitlyn was holding a carrot.

"Lipstick it is, then. Maybe Mr. Raffi Bin Najjar will give us our very own miracle."

As Caitlyn stroked the mare, she relaxed.

Only later would she wonder why she hadn't had the slightest premonition that Raffi Bin Najjar was no stranger to Wild Horse Ranch—or to her.

By the afternoon, Caitlyn had forgotten all about the need for lipstick. All it had taken for her day to spin hopelessly out of control was one phone call.

Lisa, her best friend and owner of the neighboring ranch, had sounded so desperate. "You know bees stung Ramblin' Man in his trailer last week, and he hasn't been himself. I have to move him to Mom's stud barn to cover a couple of mares, but he simply will not load. I don't know what to do. Can you help me?"

"Only if you can ride him over here, and get someone to drive the trailer to my round pen," Caitlyn had said. "Daniel's ridden off somewhere with Manuel, and I've got an important business meeting in a couple of hours with Mr. Bin Najjar's son."

"Oh, right—about your mortgage."

"Bin Najjar's driver just phoned and said they're on their way from the airport. So, I'm stuck here."

"Oh. Okay. I guess I can make that work."

So now, instead of going over her accounts, preparing for her meeting or bothering with lipstick, Caitlyn was standing in Ramblin' Man's shadowy horse trailer, holding a lead rope attached to the stallion's halter. Wild-eyed Ramblin' Man had only put a single hoof in the trailer and was staring at her as if she were a giant.

"It's okay, baby. Nothing to be scared of," Caitlyn said gently. Snapping the lead line, she backed Ramblin' Man out of the trailer before he grew more alarmed. "You were so brave to put a foot into the trailer."

When she gave the command to retreat, a relieved Ramblin' Man jerked backward and raced away. Caitlyn jumped out of the trailer and watched him run. She'd bring him back in a minute or two. He needed to build up his courage to work on what they'd already accomplished.

"Caitlyn!" Lisa squealed from the far side of the round pen. "Why didn't you tell me Luke Kilgore was your mysterious appointment?"

Caitlyn recoiled, the name of her former lover slicing her heart like a knife.

Luke? Luke, who'd left her pregnant at twenty-one?

No... Why would he show up today, of all days?

She jerked her head around and saw the tall, dark man in the flawlessly cut business suit lounging against the rail beside Lisa. The sight of him looking so virile and smolderingly masculine made her mouth go dry. Once, she had longed for Luke's return, dreamed of it. But now her dream felt like a nightmare!

Those gorgeous green eyes, the high forehead, the chiseled cheek and jaw, that classically straight nose and those mocking, sensual lips that had once kissed every inch of her body—they could belong to no one but Luke. The shock of recognition made her shiver with torrid memories.

He was as handsome as ever, but this elegantly dressed man couldn't possibly be the same bitterly ambitious cowboy she'd loved.

"What are *you* doing here?" she demanded.

"My driver said he called and confirmed. You and I have an appointment."

"*You're* Raffi Bin Najjar?"

He nodded. "I've been known to answer to that."

"What kind of man changes his name?"

"I have two names. The one I was born with and the one Hassan gave me when he asked me to be his honorary son. Hassan prefers to call me Raffi. So I let him. One of my weaknesses is indulging those I love."

"You're too old to be adopted," she said, lashing out with her words.

"Who said anything about adoption?" His lips smiled, but his eyes didn't. Obviously, he was a man of the world now.

"What exactly does it mean, then, to be an honorary son?"

"Ask Hassan. He probably made it up. Hell, for all I know I'm the only honorary son in the world." He moved away from the rail. "Sorry my showing up here is such a shock," he said.

"No, you aren't. You deliberately tricked me!"

"Think what you like."

"I don't *like* anything about this situation!"

"Maybe neither the hell do I."

Still, despite her fear and the nameless dark emotions engulfing her, his taunting, all-too-familiar, husky voice drew her, just like it had that first day when he'd stood on her porch asking if he could see her daddy because he'd needed a job and nobody else in the county would even talk to Bubba Kilgore's son. She'd been a teenager and highly susceptible to the lure of the forbidden. Her crush had lasted several years—right up until he'd gotten her pregnant and left the county for good.

Well, at twenty-six, knowing what he was and what he'd done, she should be immune to his charms.

Right. If she was so grown-up and mature, why had the pace of her heart accelerated?

Her gaze darted past him to the house. *Where was Daniel?* She hoped, *prayed* he'd stay out of sight until she got rid of Luke.

"You're looking good, Caitlyn," Luke said, but his lips didn't curve into the sexy smile that used to follow her name.

Not that she wanted it to.

"You, too," she said reluctantly. The last thing she wanted to do was flatter him. "How is this possible?" she said, motioning to him, standing in her yard.

"What? The son of the county's no-account drunk making good?"

Lisa's sudden burst of flirtatious laughter was awkward. "Don't run yourself down. You've come a long way since then, Luke. You never were anything like Bubba."

"Thanks."

"Caitlyn's told me how rich your honorary father is! And how rich *you* are!" She moistened her lips and glanced at him slyly through her long, dark eyelashes.

Luke looked away.

Caitlyn winced. Her friend's excessive interest in Luke bothered her. As did her words.

She remembered how Luke had once had a habit of making self-deprecating remarks. People laughed, as he'd intended, but she'd known his jokes had covered soul-deep shame for having Bubba as a father. Luke had always wanted to be more than he'd been. Well, now he was rich and powerful, but was he any happier?

Quickly she reminded herself that his happiness wasn't her problem. He'd jilted her and moved on to better things, more beautiful women. He'd probably never hungered for her—as she'd hungered for him.

Or had he? He did seem as keenly aware of her as she was of him, which was hatefully gratifying.

As Lisa leaned closer to him, Caitlyn insinuated herself between them. "So, you really are Raffi Bin Najjar? I did some research, but couldn't find much."

Luke pushed away from the railing and stood taller. He'd filled out, but on him, the extra weight looked good. She was sure he was made of hot, solid muscle. The thought of touching him now made her own skin heat.

"I pay people to remove stuff I don't want on the web," Luke said.

"You can do that?"

"Most of the time. I'm not a movie star, so I'm not hounded by the paparazzi unless I'm out with somebody famous."

"Like your supermodel girlfriends?"

His mouth twisted. "Jealous?"

"Of course not! But you should have told me who you were, you know."

"Why? I'm here as a favor to Hassan. Not because I want to make your life easier. For some reason, he's become fascinated by you and your affairs."

"He's been extremely helpful."

"Yes, and I want to know why. I couldn't find out if I'd tipped you off."

"He told me you once lived here, but, of course, since I didn't know who you really were, I thought nothing of it."

"I'm as curious about his motivations as you

are. Did you two talk about me the night you went to dinner in France?"

"Not much."

"Did he tell you he invited me to come that night?"

"Yes, but I didn't know who you were, so I didn't pursue it."

"I watched you through binoculars when you were working with Sahara and decided to bow out."

So, Luke had been in Deauville, too, and had deliberately rejected her. Again.

This whole situation felt like a setup. She remembered Hassan's comments at Keeneland about the color of Daniel's eyes. She remembered Hassan asking her about Daniel over dinner in Deauville. When he'd asked questions about her son, she'd thought he was merely being polite. She'd been so proud of Daniel. She'd talked way too much about him, given away too much. She'd shown Hassan pictures, and he'd stared at them for a long time, even asking if he could keep one.

Had Hassan figured out who Daniel's father was? As one of the world's richest men, he could probably find out anything he wanted to know. Of course he would be curious about his protégé's past. Had he sent Luke here to discover Daniel?

Maybe this reunion could have been avoided if she'd been more clever. But no, she'd taken Hassan's actions at face value. He'd written her a note after Keeneland, and fool that she'd been, she'd felt flattered that such a man had remembered her name. When he'd called and asked her to help with Sahara, shc'd been flattered again. And she'd needed the money too badly to question his motives. Then, once she was in France, she'd been too impressed by the glamour of his château and stables to think rationally.

"We stuck to small talk mostly," she said now, without mentioning their conservation about Daniel.

"But after taking you to dinner, he bought your mortgage. Anything happen...*after* dinner?" Luke's hot gaze slid over her slowly, causing her nerves to sizzle. Did he think she was easy because she'd been easy with him?

"Don't you dare insinuate that your...'father'

and I had an affair, because we didn't. He was nice to me. That's all."

The intensity of Luke's gaze unnerved her. "Half a million dollars nice?"

"During dinner, I told him about my ranch. We got into finances, and I was frank about my problems. I was afraid I was about to lose the ranch. He said he appreciated what I had done for Sahara and that he wanted to help me. He stunned me by saying he'd buy the mortgage and help me get back onto my feet."

"That was all there was to it? Hassan doesn't make a habit of befriending people and rescuing them."

"He calls *you* his son!"

"I saved his kid's life. Took a bullet, too. You work with Sahara an hour or two—and he buys your mortgage? I don't get it."

She hadn't, either—although she now had a few suspicions.

"I needed the money, so I took what he offered. Wouldn't anybody in my position have done the same thing? Didn't *you?*"

"He taught me a lot when I went to work for him," Luke agreed. "He opened a lot of doors."

"I'll say. Those doors must have been made of solid gold. Five years later you're a billionaire."

Ramblin' Man walked over to the trailer and stuck his nose inside. She noted his behavior, but couldn't take any satisfaction in his progress, so long as Luke was here.

"It's true. I owe him everything. And I think the only reason Hassan helped you was because of me," Luke said.

"You? I don't get it."

"Somehow he must have figured out we'd been involved. There's nothing he wouldn't do for family, and if you claimed some tie to me…"

"But I didn't."

She again remembered Hassan's comments about Daniel's eyes and she felt afraid. Still, with an air of bravado, she said, "Why don't you ask him why he helped me?"

"I did ask him. He was evasive. So, I came here to satisfy my curiosity, and because Hassan forced the issue. The fact is, this ranch is the last place I'd willingly return to. Just as you are the last person I'd help, if I had a choice. But Hassan wants to help you, and he asked me to figure out how to do it, so here we are—stuck with each other."

"Why don't you just leave?"

"And tell Hassan to keep bailing you out? No, I'm going to get to the bottom of this. I'm here to protect Hassan."

His narrowed green eyes pierced her. His sharp words stung. *She was the last person he'd help, if he had a choice.*

He was angry. Why? He'd betrayed her family, jilted her and left her pregnant, with unattractive options, while he'd reinvented himself as this arrogant, world-class businessman. What did he have to be mad about? Unless he knew about Daniel...which he didn't. At least, not yet.

Again her gaze strayed to the house, searching for Daniel.

Don't panic. Be polite. Just send him on his way—fast. How hard could it be to get rid of a man who didn't want to be here?

So much for her miracle. She was in worse trouble than before.

Caitlyn turned to Lisa. "Look, I need to talk to Luke. In private. You can work with Ramblin' Man on your own until I get back. Do a little groundwork…like I showed you before he put his foot into the trailer."

"Okay," Lisa said reluctantly, glancing at Luke.

"Follow me," Caitlyn said curtly as she un-latched a gate and headed out of the round pen. She was tired of Lisa hanging on to their every word, and there was the added danger that Lisa might blurt out something about Daniel.

Luke nodded casually to Lisa before loping after Caitlyn. "Look, if you need to get her stallion in the trailer before we talk, go ahead. I have a report from one of my CEOs that I need to read. Our meeting can wait a half hour. Lisa told me about the bees."

He'd had time for a private chitchat with Lisa before Caitlyn had seen him. Her sudden burst of jealousy infuriated her.

Caitlyn stopped in the shadow of the barn and whirled to face him. "I'm canceling our meeting."

"The hell you are. I flew all the way from London."

"I don't care if you flew in from another galaxy. You had no right to come here under false pretenses."

"I promised Hassan I'd figure out a solution to your problems."

"I don't want your help. You're too late, Luke Kilgore. Six years too late. I've made it this long without you. I can keep on making it without you."

His green eyes flamed with surprise, and fresh suspicion. "What the hell do you mean by that?"

Her hand flew to her lips and she took a step backward. She'd almost said too much. Maybe she *had* said too much. Notching her chin higher, she held her ground. "Nothing," she said. "I want you to leave! Now! You haven't been welcome here for a very long time."

"Is that so?" He glanced upward to the barn. "I remember a time when things were very different between us."

She remembered, too. They'd made wild, sweet, unforgettable love in the hayloft. Ever since, he'd haunted her dreams. Even after he'd abandoned her, he'd cast a long shadow over her marriage.

"When you were a teenager, you followed me everywhere. I couldn't load a bale of hay without finding you watching me," he said. "You damn near threw yourself at me."

"I was a young, stupid fool!" she cried, hating that she'd once made no secret of how intensely she'd felt about him.

"I was the fool. Hell, maybe I still am." He grabbed her by the waist, pulled her close. "If it's the last thing I do, I'll figure out why Hassan really sent me here. I thought he wanted me to marry the woman I'm dating, Teresa. Then suddenly he sends me here. Why?"

She jerked free of his grip because she couldn't concentrate when in his arms. "I thought he sent you to solve my money problems."

"There's another reason. I'm sure of it. You made him think we're still connected."

She shook her head in denial. "I didn't." Frantic to distract Luke, she said, "Teresa? Is she another of your gorgeous supermodels?"

"No. A countess."

In spite of the fact that his love life was no concern of hers, Caitlyn was suddenly crushingly aware of how plain and unappealing she must seem in her dusty jeans. He'd become a mega-success while she was on the verge of bankruptcy.

Only by biting her tongue until she tasted the coppery flavor of blood was she able to remain silent. Too bad that the minute she quit biting it, she lost the battle to prove she could behave like a lady.

"If she's so perfect, you'd be a fool not to propose to her!"

"She's a little young. Nineteen. I was actually considering asking her to marry me, when Hassan started in on me about coming here. Ever since he met you at Keeneland, he's asked questions about my life in Texas. He won't say why, but I think he's decided I'm still hung up on you. Well, I'm not! I don't believe in rehashing or whining about the past, and I'll do whatever it takes to convince him—even work with you on your finances."

She caught a whiff of his musky scent mingling with minty cologne, and her feminine hormones flared. "So marry your precious Teresa and prove you and I are ancient history!"

His eyes slid over her. "You don't look much like ancient history. You look as sassy as ever. So, no man's tamed you yet? Not even your husband?"

"Leave him out of this! He's dead, you know."

"I'm sorry." There was genuine regret in his deep tone. "This is a big place. In the middle of nowhere. It must get lonely out here."

Unimaginably lonely, especially at night, when the wind blew and the eaves groaned and the coyotes howled as she lay in the dark, her head spinning with money worries.

She'd lain awake, alone, for too long. But she had a ranch to run, son to raise, hence little time for fun.

Too aware of the hunger that sparked in Luke's green eyes and her own vulnerability, she took a step backward.

When he reached out and took her by the hand, she fought to pull it free. He held on tight, lifting her palm and inspecting it closely.

"You've been working hard. Too hard." The

sympathy in his voice surprised her and temporarily lessened her anger. Without thinking, she quit tugging and leaned closer to him.

What was she doing? Softening toward him? She should fight him harder, yank her hand free, but her emotions were escalating too fast to control. His tall, powerful body and his understanding intoxicated her. She'd done without a man's passion for too long. Done without *him*. If only she'd had an inkling she'd see him today, she could have steeled herself.

Instead of trying to run, she froze. His beautiful green eyes—eyes she had so adored—stared straight into hers, igniting her soul, burning away the years and the hurt and the hatred, and melting her resistance.

He lifted her callused palm to his lips and kissed it. Only then did she jerk her hand from his. "You probably prefer women with soft hands."

"I thought I did. These days I don't meet many women who work outside with animals the way you do. When I left Texas, I dated lots of women. Until I saw you working with Ramblin' Man, I thought I'd put you totally behind me.

"You were so good with him. I respect that. You looked so beautiful and wild. I wish I'd come back, at least once, to check on you. I suddenly realized I never…said goodbye."

"No…you didn't." She caught herself. "This isn't happening," she whispered, feeling shattered by his admission, by the sweetness of his kiss on her poor battered hand.

"Something sure as hell is," he muttered, sounding angry and lost. "I should have stood my ground and stayed in London."

"You could always just go."

"It's too late now. The damage is done." His eyes devoured hers. He stared straight into her soul, which had always belonged only to him. "I've seen you. I've touched you. And now I'm curious…about a lot of things."

She didn't understand the stillness that possessed her, held her. Was she in a trance? Clasped tightly against his tall, muscular body, his heat flooding her, she could barely think, barely breathe.

It was as if she were in a dream, as if she was again caught in the vortex of the youthful passion that had nearly destroyed her. For years she'd told herself she'd do it differently if she was ever faced with such temptation again.

Now, here he was.

Time to smarten up, Caitlyn.

But she lifted her head, parted her lips invitingly. Her nipples tightened into pert berries, throbbing where they brushed his shirt and felt his heat. Slowly he lowered his mouth to hers, nibbling her top lip as he'd done in the past, sucking on it, tasting it. Then she melted against him.

"Oh, God," he muttered.

Instantly, nerves tingled in her tummy. Where he was concerned, she'd always been easy. Why did he have to make her feel so good, so fast?

Sighing, she wrapped her arms around his neck, threaded her fingers in his silky hair, stood on her tiptoes and kissed him right back. He was simply too delicious to resist.

"I'm going to hate you for this," she whispered, her voice thick. "Most of all, I'm going to hate me."

"I hear you, sweetheart."

Then his tongue invaded her mouth, and sweet,

urgent needs made her arch her body into his hardness. Like a mare showing heat, excitement blazed through her. She ached with needs she'd never felt for any other man, not even her husband.

She knew what she was doing was wrong. Luke had hurt her, rejected her, hurt Daniel without even knowing Daniel existed. She hated him for all the lost years since he'd left.

And yet there were other emotions alongside the hate. Kissing him now was like coming home after living for too many years with strangers. She couldn't get enough. She wanted him to tear off her jeans, throw her over his shoulder and carry her into the barn. She wanted to open her legs and lie down in the hay with him again.

She wanted too much. She always had.

For another long second she was alone in the universe with him. Then Ramblin' Man exploded in the trailer and Lisa yelled.

As if he suddenly realized where he was and what he was doing, Luke's hands fell away. He jumped free of her with an abruptness that startled her.

Distantly, she heard Lisa soothing Ramblin' Man in the round pen.

Luke's eyes hardened, and he cursed low under his breath.

In a bewildered daze, she stared at him. More than anything, she had wanted to stay in his arms, to cling to his strength, to enjoy feeling like a woman for the first time in years.

But that was impossible now.

"Take your hands off me! Let me go!" Caitlyn whispered needlessly. The humiliating truth was that Luke had already moved away and was no longer touching her.

He was silent for what seemed an eternity.

What was he thinking? Did he have demons she knew nothing about?

"You kiss like a woman who hasn't had any in six years," he growled, glaring at her.

She stared down at the scuffed toe of her roper boots. As always, he was uncannily perceptive. The last thing she wanted him to suspect was how she'd longed for him all through the lonely years of her marriage.

"If you want it that bad, we'd better go inside,"

he said. "Or do you still prefer the loft? Frankly, it doesn't matter to me. All I want is to get you out of my system—permanently."

Feeling ashamed of her reaction to him, she lashed out at him, too. "Ditto! I don't want you touching me again—ever! I want you gone! That's what I want."

"You didn't kiss me like a woman who wants me gone, sweetheart."

"I don't know what came over me, but believe me, I want you gone."

"Well, while I figure out your finances and Hassan's motives, I'll figure out our chemistry, as well."

"No! You're going to forget that stupid kiss and go—now."

"And if I go, how will you solve your money problems?"

"I'm too upset to think about that."

"Well, you'd better think about it."

"I can't work with you."

"You'd better adjust your attitude, because you don't have a choice."

Looking every bit as upset as she felt, he shoved

a lock of thick black hair back from his brow. "Tell you what. I'll leave…for tonight, so you can adjust to the idea of me being around. But I'll be gone for one night only. Then I'm moving in until we get this mystery solved and your mess figured out. You're fifty miles from town, and, after tonight, I don't want to waste time commuting. You'll need to make up a spare bedroom for me."

"The hell you say! Do you think I would let you move into my house after what just happened? I don't want you in this state!"

"Do you really want me to tell Hassan you won't work with me?"

Of course not. And Luke knew it.

"Because I will," he said. "If I tell him to pull the plug on you, he'll do it."

She shook her head, not wanting to believe that.

"The ranch and your horse operation will be history. I could convince him to sell everything at auction. You know what that means."

Yes. She knew. There was such a weak market for her horses, that several would be euthanized or sold to meat packers.

"Hassan would never…"

"I think I know him better than you do. He wants to help you, but if you refuse his help you will leave him no choice but to make unpleasant decisions. Do you want to lose the ranch again, like your daddy did?" he continued. "Only, this time there won't be a rich idiot like Robert Wakefield to marry and give it back to you."

"I haven't lost it yet, thank you very much! You're only rich because of your connections to Hassan. Well, I know the real you, and maybe I don't think you're so great. My mother warned me that you were just like Bubba."

Her mother had fired Luke because he was a thief. Cait hadn't wanted to believe he'd stolen cash out of her father's truck, but when Luke had never returned or contacted her to contradict her mother's claim, the truth of his betrayal had seemed self-evident.

"So, you believed her?" Something flashed in his eyes. Was it pain? Or rage? "You're wrong," he said. "You don't know me at all. You never did. And I didn't know you, either, or I would never have been fool enough to mistake you for a sweet, innocent girl and fall in love with you."

His startling admission flashed through her like lightning. He'd never admitted he loved her, and she wasn't about to believe him now. Believing him would only soften her heart toward him.

Love. He didn't know the meaning of the word.

"Leave," she whispered.

Much to her surprise, he nodded. "Like I said… I'm going…for now. I intend to spend the afternoon talking to your accountant. I had hoped to take you with me, but it seems our new business arrangement is going to take some getting used to."

He spun on his heel and strode toward the long black limo parked in front of her house.

If only this would be the last she'd ever see of him. But he'd be back tomorrow, and while he was in town there was no telling what people might tell him about Daniel, especially if he asked the right questions. There had been talk at the time of her marriage—talk that had never completely died.

Even if no one talked, if Luke moved in, he'd

see Daniel on a daily basis. There was no way she could keep the truth a secret for long.

Better that she control how he found out.

She shut her eyes and sucked in a breath. She had to tell him the truth herself.

"Wait!" She ran after his tall, broad-shouldered figure.

He turned and regarded her so coldly, a chill traced down her spine. How would she ever find the courage to tell him he had a son? But she had to. Period.

"I'll meet you in town…a little later…after I finish working with Ramblin' Man," she said. "What time's your appointment?"

He told her.

She licked her lips and said she'd be there thirty minutes late. "After we get through talking with Bruce, there's something I need to tell you. Something personal," she whispered awkwardly, staring anywhere but at him. "It's very important. Maybe we could have coffee at Jean's Butterchurn. We can talk privately there."

His eyes narrowed. "This isn't going to be good news, is it?"

"I guess that will depend on how you take it," she said. "It's not altogether bad news, but it's certainly not something I relish telling you."

Then she shook herself and stood straighter. No matter how much she dreaded her hour of confession, she wasn't going to give him the satisfaction of seeing how afraid she was.

"Well, I've got a stallion to load," she said briskly.

"Later, then." He turned and headed to his limo.

Two

What the hell did she have to tell him that was so important?

It wasn't the first time she'd fed him that line. On the day he'd left for good, nearly six years ago, she'd told him she had something important to tell him. But when he'd gone to meet her in their secret place, her mother had showed up instead. Her mother had fired him and set him straight about a lot of other things, too. Caitlin planned to marry someone else.

Luke had left, but later when he'd calmed down, he'd called Caitlyn. She'd never answered his calls, so he'd written. She'd never written back. Clearly, she'd wanted him out of her life but had lacked the courage to break up with him in person.

Who cared what she had to say today? Quit thinking about it, he told himself.

As if he could. Her brown eyes had been huge, fear-filled dark orbs, her shaky tone ominous. He'd wanted to reach out and pull her close. Thank goodness he hadn't acted on that rash impulse. She didn't deserve his kindness, nor his compassion. She never had.

They say you can never go home.

As he'd told Caitlyn, Luke damn sure wouldn't have come here if he'd had a choice. He belonged in London, in his office, sitting at the helm of his many businesses.

But Hassan, to whom he owed everything, had prevailed.

For nearly six years, Luke Kilgore had avoided all things Texan, especially its women. He wanted no one with dark hair or fiery dark eyes that held a hint of vulnerability; he wanted no one with a soft drawl that sounded too much like a cat's purr.

Now, sprawled in the back of his leased stretch

limo on this fool's errand, trying to pretend he was relaxed, Luke's fingers clenched, wrinkling the latest of his CEO's reports about Kommstarr's disgruntled employees. Luke thrust it aside impatiently. Steve's figures in defense of his out-of-control expenditures at Kommstarr made no sense. Luke didn't like firing people any better than Steve did, but some cuts had to be made.

Hell, Luke had hardly been able to concentrate since he'd landed in San Antonio last night and felt the warmth, even in winter, of the vast, starlit Texas sky. So different from London's gray, damp chill that all he'd been able to think about was *her*. In his hotel in downtown San Antonio he'd even dreamed of her.

Why was she scared?

Caitlyn Cooper Wakefield.

Now that he'd seen her, touched her, tasted her, she'd scrambled his brain just like she'd done in the past. How could she still get to him?

Six years ago she'd merely been Caitlyn Cooper. A respected rancher's only daughter. She should have been off-limits to the motherless son of the county's number one drunk, Bubba Kilgore. She would have been—if she'd obeyed her daddy or if Luke had had enough sense to keep his hands off her.

Luke compared the woman she was now to the slim girl she'd been back then. She'd been more cute than beautiful, with a freckled nose and wide, dark, innocent eyes that had sparkled with curiosity and laughter. And she'd laughed a lot. At least, in his company.

She hadn't laughed today.

Back then she'd seemed to find him as exciting as he'd found her. From that first afternoon, when he'd stomped onto her daddy's porch, desperate for a job, and she'd refused to invite him in, there had been vital chemistry between them.

She wasn't nearly as beautiful as the women he dated now, and she didn't dress as fashionably. She'd never cared about those things. Deep down he admired her because she wasn't vain. Her face was narrow and angular, her thick black hair unruly. She hadn't worn any makeup. Did it matter? There was something real, something genuine about her, and she sure as hell knew how to kiss.

He wished he could forget how seductively soft and warm her lips had felt beneath his own, forget how good she'd tasted, forget how hard he'd become even before he'd grabbed her this afternoon. Lacking polish, she was all fire and sass, making him burn.

Her hands had climbed his chest and wrapped around his neck as if she knew she belonged to him and no one else. When she'd leaned into him and pulled him close, he'd felt the heat of every female curve.

She'd been hotter than ever, maybe because she'd known exactly what she wanted. Or maybe she'd missed him…really missed him, as he'd missed her.

Like the kiss today, the memory of the long-ago evening when he'd made love to her still had the power to sear him. He hadn't gone looking for trouble that evening, but it sure as hell found him.

He'd knocked on her door, looking for her daddy. He'd needed an advance against his wages since Bubba had drunk up the rent. She'd come to the door in tight shorts that skimmed her curvy bottom and said, "Maybe he's in the barn."

Only, she'd known he wasn't when she'd followed Luke out there, closing the big, heavy doors behind her, calling to him across the dark in that raspy purr of hers. Then she'd undone her hair so that it tumbled around her shoulders. When she'd held out her arms and told him she loved him, he'd tried to talk some sense into her, even as his heart thundered.

"You don't know what you're doing, girl," he'd warned.

"But I've always known how I feel," she whispered, "ever since I first saw you."

"You're too young to know anything. Folks around here think I'm nothing."

"I don't care. I don't want to go my whole life wanting you like this…and never having had you." She moved toward him. "Just once. That's all I'm asking for."

"No one can know," he said.

"Nobody but us," she'd whispered, sliding into his arms, her soft curves melting against his hard muscles.

She'd felt right, perfect.

"Just us," he'd murmured, kissing her passionately.

For him, that time with her had been special. No other woman had ever come close to mattering so much. But then, no other woman had used her mother to throw him out like he was nothing. That had been equally hard to forget.

Had she just wanted to scratch an itch? Had she known then she would have to marry Wakefield if she wanted to get her precious ranch back? For years Luke had tormented himself with those questions.

She'd been the first girl he'd loved—and she'd be the last. She'd taught him love held a dark power. She'd taught him there were worse things than having a mean old man for a father. She'd taught him there were worse things than being born poor. She'd taken a hatchet to his heart and soul.

Swearing she loved him, she'd given herself to him on a bed of hay that night in the barn. Then, as soon as she could, she'd married Robert

Wakefield, no doubt because he was the son of the banker who'd repossessed her family's ranch.

But life had a way of being messy, and nothing had worked out as she'd planned. Robert had died. The ranch was in trouble again, and she was a struggling widow with a son.

A son. Funny that he hadn't seen the kid. Not that he wanted to see Wakefield's kid, who was living proof that she'd been with another man these past six years.

Some people were good at letting go. Luke envied them. Not that he didn't go through the motions of a man who'd moved on. He owned a glamorous penthouse in London. Invitations to his parties were sought after. He dated the most beautiful women in Europe. Except for his friend Nico Romano, an Italian prince with an independent wife from Texas, his married male business associates said they envied Luke his carefree life.

Although he didn't pick up the report again, Luke barely spared a glance out the tinted windows. He didn't have to. The harsh brown scrubland was deeply engraved into his consciousness.

He'd accomplish this errand for Hassan as quickly as possible. Then he'd figure out once and for all what was behind Hassan's obsessive interest in Caitlyn.

Not that he hadn't tried to find out after Hassan had met her at Keeneland. When Luke hadn't reacted to the Wakefield name, Hassan had pressed, asking him if he'd known Caitlyn Wakefield personally.

"Yes, I worked for her father."

"And? Did you care for her?"

"It doesn't matter. Her mother fired me. I left Texas and never saw any of them again. Why do you want to know?"

"You don't talk about Texas much."

"I'm not all that proud of who I was in Texas, or of how people treated me. It's something I've tried to put behind me."

He'd thought that was the end of it. Then Hassan had asked Caitlyn to help him with Sahara and had invited Luke to Deauville without telling him he'd hired Caitlyn as Sahara's trainer. When Luke had seen her working with the stallion, he'd asked Hassan again why he was so interested in her. It would have been so much easier to use a world-class French trainer instead of bringing Caitlyn from the States.

Again, Hassan had been evasive, saying only that her advice had saved him from making a particularly disastrous purchase.

"Why did you invite me to dine with the two of you?" Luke had asked. "It's as if you are determined to get us together."

"Sometimes we are rash in our youth. Sometimes it's a mistake to lose touch with old friends."

"Not in this case."

"You could be wrong, my son."

"Well, I won't come for dinner if you insist on including her."

"I do insist on her presence tonight."

"Then I'll pass."

"You shall be missed, my son."

Hassan's stubborn behavior and fascination with Caitlyn made no sense, but Luke would get to the bottom of it. Then, hopefully, within the week, he'd be home with Teresa.

Luke saw a flash of movement out the window. A handsome blood bay horse, ridden by a small figure, sprang across the road right in front of the limo. The driver honked and hit the brakes too fast and too hard. The bay spooked and started bucking.

Tires squealing, the limo fishtailed in a swirl of gravel, sliding to a standstill in front of a prickly pear cactus. The pages of Steve's report came loose and flew all over the limo's plush interior.

The riderless red horse plunged wildly away from the veils of dust near the car, racing across the depopulated landscape. Then he stopped and circled back, staring at something on the ground. When the dust settled, Luke saw a small boy lying still and lifeless on the road.

Luke leaped out of the limo at the same moment as his driver.

"I didn't see him, sir! Not until it was nearly too late!"

"It wasn't your fault," Luke assured the man.

"He came out of nowhere."

"See to the car." Luke strode toward the prostrate boy, who'd stirred at the sound of their voices.

A cowboy came running from the pasture. "The boy, he got away from me, señor."

When the kid moaned, Luke felt some of his tension ease. The car hadn't hit the boy. He'd just been bucked. Maybe he was okay. At the same age, Luke had ridden just as recklessly and had taken many a hard fall without doing permanent damage. In some ways, kids were tougher than adults.

Careless of the fine wool and silk blend of his custom-made suit, Luke knelt on the ground beside the boy.

The kid groaned and sat up, blinking at him suspiciously. The boy's red-checked cowboy shirt was torn in two places. He raised a quick, thin hand to shade his tanned brow, squinting at the brilliant afternoon sun coming from behind Luke. The boy's lips parted in a gap-toothed grin.

"You okay…?" Luke began, feeling a jolt of recognition.

"Sorry, mister. I…"

The kid had jet black hair and green eyes— green eyes that were the exact same shade as his own.

Luke's gut twisted. Emerald eyes stared straight into his for an endless moment, during which Luke felt something near his heart shift.

Luke didn't believe in coincidences, and Hassan placed an inordinate value on sons. Was this boy the answer? Did Hassan think…?

Had Hassan seen Caitlyn's son and noticed the resemblance to Luke? Had Hassan met the boy at Keeneland?

Suddenly Luke couldn't breathe. It was as if a band had wrapped around his chest and squeezed. In a weird panic—he never panicked—he fought to ignore dozens of questions that bombarded his stunned mind.

"I asked you if you're okay?" Luke's voice was hard and strange, unrecognizable. "Anything hurt? Broken? Are you dizzy?"

The kid felt real. The rest of his life—London, Teresa, his businesses, his unstoppable ambition, even Hassan—belonged to a dream that had nothing to do with his life, which was here.

"I'm fine, but I've got to catch that damn Demon before he bolts for the barn and I have to walk all the way back."

"Don't cuss."

"Sorry!"

The kid didn't look the least bit sorry as he sat up and got ready to spring to his feet.

Luke put a hand on his shoulder. "Not so fast. Why don't you sit here a minute or two, catch your breath."

"I said I'm okay," the boy protested impatiently, looking defiant.

Just as Luke would have done at the same age.

"Right. And I say it's too soon to be so sure. What's your name?"

"Daniel." His bottom lip curling, the kid stared at the ground.

"You got a last name?"

"'Course I do! Wakefield." There was fierce pride in his low tone, the kind of pride Luke had never felt for his biological father. When the kid tried unsuccessfully to shake loose from Luke's iron grip, his bottom lip grew even more prominent.

"My name's Luke Kilgore."

"Glad to meet you, Mr. Kilgore," Daniel said automatically.

"Glad to meet you, too."

The boy on the ground didn't look a thing like the blond, blue-eyed Wakefield bunch. Luke's mind raced backward.

"How old are you, Daniel?" Luke asked slowly, as unwanted pressure pounded in his temples.

This couldn't be happening. But it was. The angry kid looked just like *he'd* looked at the same age.

"Five."

The number was a sucker punch in the gut.

Damn her. Was this why she had married Wakefield so quickly? Had she been pregnant? Had she slept with them both and hoped to pass off his baby as the wealthier Wakefield's to get the ranch back? Had she despised the thought she might be carrying a Kilgore?

Luke clenched and unclenched his fists. When one speculated, one was usually wrong. What mattered now was finding out the truth.

"Does your mother know where you are?" Luke asked in a low, even tone. "That you were riding Demon bareback?"

The kid tensed and then lowered his eyes guiltily. "Sure. I was with Manuel, so it's okay."

"Right," Luke said softly. "What do you say we catch Demon so the two of you can run along home, back to the ranch, so your mother won't worry?"

"She's not worrying. She's too busy getting ready for her meeting with some guy."

"That would be me."

"Oh. Are you rich? Some car, huh? Long." His eyes lit up. "Like a bus."

"Not exactly. It's called a limousine. Limo for short. What do you say we catch your horse?"

Luke and Daniel stood up together, and Manuel joined them. Demon's ears shot forward and he whinnied. As Luke and the boy dusted themselves off, the blood bay gelding hung his head and licked his lips.

Good sign, Luke thought as Manuel slowly approached the horse.

The well-proportioned gelding didn't run away. He stood docilely, allowing Manuel to retrieve the reins. Manuel swung himself onto the horse. Then Luke lifted Daniel up to the mounted man.

A shadow passed over Daniel's face as he looked down. "I got you all dirty. You're gonna tell Mom on me."

"I'm not sure what I'll say to her. But I'll catch up to you two at the house," Luke said, his tone hard as he dusted himself off again.

"Did you come to buy a horse or something?" the kid asked.

"Or something."

"Good, 'cause me and Mom could sure use the money."

Money—had she married Wakefield because his daddy had been a banker and he'd owned Wild Horse Ranch? Or to give her baby a name?

When had she learned she was pregnant? Was her pregnancy the reason she hadn't taken his calls or answered his letters?

"See you," Daniel said, dismissing Luke casually.

Then the boy leaned forward with the ease of a natural rider. Soon boy, man and horse were cantering down the shoulder of the road while Luke stood still and silent, watching them.

Luke identified with that half-wild kid. Almost

as if Luke was riding Demon himself, he felt the calves of those thin legs gripping the powerful animal. They were his legs, his knees squeezing tight, his lean body leaning forward, his hands lightly holding the reins. It was him urging the great creature faster, faster, until the ride became exhilarating.

"Breathe, Daniel. Don't forget to breathe," Luke whispered.

Then horse, boy and man were flying, airborne, united, and Luke's own soul rushed after them. He hadn't felt this alive in years.

What if the kid was his son?

No sooner had the trio melted into the haze of the horizon than a knot of longing formed in Luke's throat. Should he have let Daniel back on the beast so soon? The boy had said he was fine, and he was with Manuel. But was the boy okay? What if he had a concussion?

Acute parental anxiety was new to him and made him feel foolish. The kid probably wasn't even his. But whether he was or he wasn't, Luke's concern caused beads of sweat to break out on his brow.

Had Caitlyn wanted him gone so he wouldn't find out about Daniel? Was that why she'd been afraid? If so, she was far more deceptive than he'd believed.

Luke wanted answers, and he wanted them now. Grabbing his cell, he punched in Hassan's number. It was probably midnight Hassan's time, but Luke didn't give a damn.

As always, Hassan's voice was warm with paternal interest in a way that Luke's biological father's never had been.

"Raffi. You had a safe journey? No problems?"

"Only one. I just met Daniel."

There was a long silence before Hassan finally spoke. "I saw him at Keeneland. He looked so much like you."

"Why didn't you tell me?"

"I was right? He *is* yours, then?"

Three

As soon as his limo had returned to Caitlyn's ranch and braked in front of the house, Luke flung open his door. He felt torn by the conflicting emotions raging inside him. He wished he'd never come to Texas; he was glad he'd come. He wished Hassan had leveled with him from the beginning; he was glad he'd seen the boy with his own eyes. He was furious at Caitlyn and yet filled with tenderness for her bravely defiant little son. He was in such an irrational state, he knew she was the last person he needed to talk to, but he wanted her to know that if the kid was theirs, he wouldn't walk away from her or Daniel.

"The boy looked so much like you," Hassan had said over the phone. "I couldn't forget about him and do nothing. That is why I helped her. That is why I sent you and nobody else. If you are family, so are they."

"You could have told me."

"I was so struck by him when I saw him, I knew you would be, too. I know what it is…to nearly lose a son. I wanted you to see him for yourself. To be struck by him as I was."

Oh, Luke felt struck, all right.

"There are some things a man must see and feel for himself, decide for himself," Hassan had said.

Fisting his hands, Luke stormed toward the round pen and frowned when he found Lisa instead of Caitlyn. The young woman leaned against a railing, watching and listening to the commotion in her gooseneck trailer.

"Where's Caitlyn?" he demanded.

"Ah, back so soon." Lisa batted her long eyelashes boldly as she fingered the falls at the end of her quirt.

"Caitlyn better not be in that trailer with your horse!"

Her brows snapped together. Sucking in a miffed breath, she quit fiddling with her quirt. "Why not? She knows what she's doing. Why, she's almost got Ramblin' Man loaded. And in record time. He can be a brute, that one."

Luke's fury and impatience vanished. The thought of Caitlyn in that tiny trailer with a huge, unpredictable stallion that had to weigh well over a thousand pounds made his gut clench. Was she suicidal? He wanted to scream at her to get the hell out of there, but of course he couldn't do that without endangering her even more. So, instead, he moved soundlessly around the pen, taking a circuitous route so as not to spook the stallion. He'd wait behind the trailer until she'd safely loaded the horse.

When he reached his destination and she still hadn't come out, his heart began to thud more forcefully. Then he heard her soothing voice, along with the nervous clatter of Ramblin' Man's hooves.

Why couldn't the beast just load?

"No bees today," she was saying in that feather-soft purr. "Nothing for a big boy like you to be scared of. Come on, baby, just one more step and you can go home. Don't you want to go home?"

And then Luke's cell phone rang.

Before Luke could shut it off, the horse had exploded, his head banging into the roof, which caused him to react even more wildly. Hooves banged. Caitlyn screamed. Ramblin' Man, his eyes round, burst from the trailer faster than a rocket off a launchpad, dragging Caitlyn behind him by a slender foot. Somehow she'd gotten tangled in the longe line.

Easy to do in such tight, dimly lit quarters, he thought grimly.

With a cry of sheer terror, Lisa leaped out of the round pen so she could watch the drama from the other side of the railing without risking her own neck.

It had been a while since Luke had dealt directly with horses, but he remembered that when a fifteen-hundred-pound horse wanted to take one step, five men against his chest couldn't stop him. Ramblin' Man wanted out of the pen, and if somebody didn't get him under control, he'd trample Caitlyn or drag her to death first.

Without a thought for his own hide, Luke placed both hands on the railing and threw himself into the pen. Yelling to Lisa to throw him her quirt, he caught it on the run and raced toward the horse.

Thankfully, Manuel sprang into the pen alongside him. With the other man's expert help, Luke soon grabbed the double-braided marine rope Caitlyn had been using as a longe line. With it and the quirt, he took charge. Applying pressure, he soon had Ramblin' Man's attention and respect.

"Stay where you are," he ordered Manuel. Ramblin' Man had heeded a few commands and had stopped to stare at them, so Luke handed Manuel the heavy, webbed line. "Keep his attention focused on you while I free her."

Manuel nodded grimly and clucked to the horse.

Not wanting to spook Ramblin' Man further, Luke walked slowly to Caitlyn. She was sitting up by the time he reached her, tugging fiercely at the line around her ankle.

Before he could hunker down beside her, she'd

snatched the line loose and was glaring at him as if everything was his fault—which, unfortunately, it was.

"Were you trying to kill me? Is that your idea of a solution, Kilgore? There was a time when you knew a thing or two about horses."

He still did. He owned a stable, and several of its horses were champions.

"I'm sorry," he muttered. "I was upset about something else and I forgot about my damn cell phone."

"City slicker!"

"I said I was sorry."

"Well, don't just stand there gaping at me, give me a hand up before somebody else calls you and Ramblin' Man finishes what he started."

Luke pulled her to her feet, but no sooner had she put her weight on her ankle than she gave a cry that pierced his heart. Damn it. Against his will, he cared about this woman.

Crumpling against him, she cursed under her breath, coupling his name with several colorful invectives that would have made him laugh under different circumstances.

"Let me go!" she yelled.

"If I do, you'll fall on your delectable ass!"

"Anything's preferable to being in your arms!"

"Hey, you jumped me this time," he said, grabbing her.

"Did not!"

Pulling her closer, he swung her into his arms. "You're not walking on that foot till we figure out what's wrong with it."

"You can't tell me what to do."

"Just you watch me."

When she began pushing at his wide shoulders, he ignored her puny struggles and carried her toward the gate with long, even strides.

"Open it," he commanded.

"The hell you say. Put me down this minute."

"In the house. On your bed. Not until. Unless you enjoy lounging around in my arms, you'll open the damn gate."

When she hesitated, he whispered against her earlobe, "Your choice. I can stand here all day. Hell, I'm beginning to think you're stalling so I'll kiss you again."

As his mouth descended toward hers, she moved

her head away from his. Unloosing more highly creative curses, she grumpily lifted the catch. Then she crossed her arms over her breasts and endured his carrying her to the house in stony silence. This time, when he'd climbed the stairs to her porch and stopped at the front door, she reached out and twisted the doorknob.

"Where's your bedroom?" he asked. They stood in the living room, which was filled with pictures of her parents and Daniel. As usual, her dominating mother was frowning in every shot. Funny, there wasn't a single shot of Robert, Cait's beloved, belated husband. Again, Luke wondered why she'd married the other man so quickly after Luke had left. She'd seemed so madly in love with him, Luke was no longer sure he believed her mother's version of the story.

"Just put me on the sofa and go."

"Don't make me ask again."

"Down the hall. First door on the right."

When he finally laid her down on her rumpled bed, she moaned—maybe from the pain in her ankle, maybe from exasperation that she had to deal with him—and he felt an unwanted twinge of sympathy.

"I'd better take a look at that ankle," he whispered, his deep tone uncustomarily gentle.

To his surprise she didn't object, although she did wince when he unzipped her boot and removed it. Taking great care not to hurt her any more than he had to, he examined her ankle, slowly moving it in circles, first one way and then the other.

She grimaced. "You know, this foot play isn't my idea of fun!"

"Nor mine."

Pearly dots of perspiration dotted her brow. "So, how much longer are you going to do this?" she said through gritted teeth.

"You have full range of motion. I think we should ice it."

"There's a bag of peas in the freezer. Bottom shelf."

"Okay. Can I get you anything else? A glass of water?"

She shook her head. "After you get me that sack of peas, I'd like for you to go back to London."

"You're going to need some help around here."

"Not from the likes of you."

Ignoring that dig, he went to the kitchen, returning swiftly with the peas, which he pressed against her ankle. "Now, if you'll give me the name of your doctor, I'll call him for you. You need to have your ankle checked out by a medical professional as soon as possible."

"Haven't you done enough damage for one day? I want you gone. Lisa can help me with the rest."

As if on cue, the front door banged open, and Lisa called out to her.

"Lisa!" Caitlyn yelled, sounding panicky. "Back here."

"Mom?" Daniel cried. The boy's flying footsteps resounded in the hall as he raced ahead of Lisa and slammed into the bedroom. "Mom!" he began breathlessly. "Oh, Mr. Kilgore? You're still here." He suddenly looked doubly anxious.

Daniel had changed into a white shirt, so there was no evidence of his fall.

When Luke's knowing gaze locked on Caitlyn's face, she whitened. Noticing that she was fisting and unfisting the top edge of her sheet, Luke sank down onto the bed beside her. He couldn't believe it, but he almost felt sorry for her.

Leaning closer, he whispered, "You and I have a lot more to talk about than your financial mess, don't we? Or am I wrong about Daniel being the real reason you're so anxious to get rid of me?"

"How did you know his name?"

"I met him a while ago. He's the reason I came back so fast."

She closed her eyes and swallowed hard. "This isn't happening."

"So, is he mine?" Luke murmured even more softly against her ear.

Her eyes widened with guilty alarm.

"Is he?" Luke repeated, determined to make her answer.

She closed her eyes, and lifted her chin up and down ever so slightly.

"Thought so," he whispered. "You've got a lot of explaining to do…when we're alone."

She stiffened. "I was going to tell you," she said in a voice too low for Lisa to overhear. "This afternoon."

"Right."

"I was!"

He stared through her.

"This doesn't have to change anything," she murmured tightly.

"Are you out of your mind?" he whispered.

"You said this was the last place you wanted to be."

"That was before my little run-in with Daniel. Now, I want to know how this happened, and why you never bothered to inform me."

"You were gone, remember? Robert was here. And now? A man like you couldn't possibly want any permanent ties to me or him or this place."

Luke remembered his mother leaving and how awful he'd felt without her. It was unacceptable to think of Daniel growing up without both his parents, if possible.

"You don't know a damn thing about what I want. Apparently you never did. But I'll give you a real big clue—Daniel changes everything."

Lisa was frowning, her intent gaze never leaving their faces.

Curious as well, Daniel tiptoed nearer. "Why

are you in bed when it's daytime? Are you hurt, Mom? Or sick…like Daddy?" His voice thinned. "Why is Mr. Kilgore still here? Why are you both whispering?"

Forcing a weak smile, Caitlyn reached out and smoothed Daniel's dark, tousled hair. "It's just my ankle. I got tangled up in the longe line. I'll be fine in no time."

"Since it's all my fault that your mother was hurt, I'm going to stay here to help you all out till she's better," Luke said.

"No…" Caitlyn sputtered.

"Don't be ridiculous, Cait! Why, I think that's real generous of you, Luke," Lisa said. "It'll be a pleasure having you around."

"The pleasure's all mine," Luke drawled.

Daniel's face relaxed. Sighing heavily, he agreed, "Good. 'Cause I was really, really scared. I fell off Demon today, and Mr. Kilgore helped me remount. Did he tell you about it, Mom?"

"No. Not yet," Caitlyn said.

"Good, 'cause I thought maybe I was in trouble. That's why I was hiding."

"He fell off that horse, and you knew it!" Her eyes flew to Luke. "Why didn't you tell me?"

"Believe me, I would have, if Ramblin' Man hadn't exploded the way he did. Meeting Daniel was weighing heavily on my mind. That's why I didn't think about my phone when I was waiting for you to finish in the trailer."

Her slim hand froze in Daniel's. "I see," she whispered. "Honey, could you go out into the living room for a second with Miss Lisa while I talk to Mr. Kilgore privately?"

"But can't I just stay while you talk—"

"No."

"Please. Just for a second."

"He and I have some business to discuss."

"But I won't listen!" Refusing to budge, Daniel crossed his arms over his thin chest and curled his lip. Luke could see that the kid did as he pleased a lot of the time. Not always a good thing.

"Daniel!" she said sharply.

"You're not going to sell Demon to him, are you?"

"No. Just some big-people talk that would bore you."

"I won't interrupt," he said, inching closer to her.

"You heard her, so don't argue. Just go," Luke said in a voice that was both firm and kind. "We'll be through in no time. Then you can stay with your mom for as long as you like."

Daniel nodded and got up. "Can I have a cookie?"

"Lisa, do you think maybe you could find a snack for Daniel?" Luke asked.

Lisa, who had been hanging on to every word, reluctantly took Daniel's arm and led him down the hall. "Sure thing. Daniel, how about some milk and cookies?"

"Only one, Lisa," Caitlyn said. "Sugar makes him hyper."

"Can I have chocolate chip…?"

"If you have any," Lisa said.

"In the freezer," Cait said.

Forgetting his mother, Daniel ran down the hall to check the cookie jar.

Luke got up and closed the door. When he went back to her bed, Caitlyn grabbed his wrist and pulled him closer. Warmth flashed through him. Then, realizing she was touching him, she yanked her hand away as if she, too, felt the burn.

He held his breath for a charged second, far from unscathed by the feral need she still aroused in him so easily. He wasn't over her. He wanted her. He'd never wanted another more than he wanted her.

"Don't tell him who you are. Do you hear me? Because you're not his father. Not in any way that matters."

Because of you!

He was angry, but it was still all too easy to imagine her at nineteen, pregnant with his child and enduring her strict, critical mother's censure. Had she been afraid to confess the baby was his? If she'd made some bad decisions, so had he. He should have returned to check on her. Maybe she would have told him about the baby. Well, it was too late to change the past, but that didn't mean he couldn't change the future.

"Let's get something straight. If he's mine, I intend to be a father to him in the future— whether you like it or not."

"He's yours, I guess, but only biologically," she snapped.

"Then he's mine. Period. I can see he needs a father, too. He has way too much freedom to do as he pleases."

"Don't you judge me! There's a lot you don't understand. Daniel is upset because the man he believed to be his father is dead. There's no way he could handle discovering who you really are."

"Maybe not right now.... I have no intention of telling him until he's more accustomed to me. I'll know when the time is right."

"He blames himself for Robert's death. He'd run off and had all of us scared to death. Robert had been ill for a while, and I was overwrought about that. When Daniel finally showed up that afternoon, I'm afraid I said some things that really upset him. Then Robert died suddenly, before any of us thought he would, and Daniel blamed himself. I've told Daniel it was Robert's illness that killed him, not anything Daniel did. But I don't think he believes me."

"Poor little guy. That's a heavy load for a young kid," Luke said. "I can see he's had a rough time."

"Yes, he has—thanks in part to you."

"That from the woman who never bothered to inform me of his existence."

"You were supposed to meet me that afternoon. You left without even bothering to say goodbye."

"Had I done that, I would deserve your anger. But that's not the way it was, and you damn well—"

She interrupted him. "You were already gone when I found out for sure!"

"I wrote and told you where I was. I called. You never answered. You married Wakefield!"

"You called?" She scowled at him in confusion, probably for reminding her of how badly she'd treated him. No doubt once she'd made up her mind to marry for the ranch, she'd decided never to look back. She'd considered him collateral damage and nothing more.

Casting blame for the past accomplished nothing. What he did to resolve their present problem was all that mattered. He heaved in a breath. "I don't like remembering you or what happened between us any better than you do. So, okay, hate my guts to your heart's content, and let me hate yours. But there's something you need to understand. A simple DNA test will prove he's mine. As his father, I could fight for custody. With my money I could make your life a living hell. I intend to know my son—with or without your permission. So we can work together, or you can fight me. It's your choice."

"Don't you dare use your money to threaten me! Just because I'm a woman who's temporarily down on her luck, you think you hold all the cards. Well, you don't! He's mine, and I love him. And he loves me."

"I know that. I respect that. But I want to be part of his life, too. Is that so unreasonable?"

"Under the circumstances, yes! You live in London, and we live here."

"Geography."

"I have a ranch—here."

"You could relocate…nearer to me. You can raise Thoroughbreds anywhere."

"Why would I do that? I read about the shallow, materialistic life you lead, the beautiful women, the wealth…. I don't want Daniel influenced by a man who'll teach him that women are disposable playthings."

"That's not what I'll teach him. And for the record, I'm too busy *working* to see all the women the gossips say I see. You don't know me well enough to pass judgment."

Maybe he hadn't really known *himself* until this moment. Although his life was filled with all the so-called right people and things, his loneliness was profound. It was as if long ago he'd lost some vital piece of himself. At times when he thought he should be content, he felt restless instead. In such moments he always wondered what it was that he could possibly need to complete his life.

Coming back here—seeing Caitlyn and then Daniel—had changed him. For the first time in a long time, he felt driven by something true rather than by anger or the ambition to prove himself. He had a son. He was determined to be a father. He'd been hasty when he'd let Caitlyn's mother speak for her.

"I'm going to change my lifestyle," he said. "This has made me realize it's time I settled down."

"All because of Daniel?"

"Absolutely."

"Why should I believe you?"

"I don't care what you believe. All you need to know is that I intend to get to know him and be his father. Thus, I'll be staying here, with you, indefinitely. Like I said before—if I were you, I'd cooperate."

"What about your work, your life, your countess in London?"

"Much as I appreciate your concern, I'll figure out a way to make my plan work."

"But nobody's invited you to stay. Nobody wants you."

Her words sent a chill through him as he remembered his loveless childhood. He'd had no mother, a trashed house and a father who'd been almost worse than no father. The whole county, including Caitlyn's mother, had called Bubba Kilgore trash and thought that Luke was no better.

Well, he had money and prestige now, lots of it, and he had Hassan's paternal love. Teresa, who had the pedigree and the polish he lacked, wanted to marry him. All he had to do was ask her. Had he hesitated to propose because she was too young, or because, deep down, even with Teresa at his side, he often felt alienated in this luxurious life he'd built?

Strangely, he felt more grounded with Caitlyn. Was it because they shared the same roots? Or because his feelings for her went deeper than he'd let himself believe?

He would stay here and help Caitlyn. He didn't care what he had to do or say to get his way. Since he'd been born in the gutter, he could sink to her level no matter how low she went.

Thus, his voice was very hard when he spoke to her again. "Would you really send your son's biological father away when he's the only man who can pull your sweet little ass out of the financial mess you've made? If you're destitute, what will happen to Daniel? The day might come, sooner than you think, when you'll beg me to take him."

"Never!"

"You'd prefer him to starve? I always thought mothers wanted what's best for their children."

"Of course I want what's best! I just don't think

you're it!" She lunged at him, but the movement was ill considered and it twisted her ankle in the sheets. She cried out in pain and collapsed against her pillow, her thin face ashen.

His fury forgotten, he sank down beside her again, hating himself for having made such unreasonable threats in the heat of anger. "Are you okay?"

"Yes," she whispered, shaking, closing her eyes to shut out the pain. Or maybe to shut him out.

"I'd better call your doctor," he said, as he gently replaced the frozen peas on her foot. "What's his name?"

In that same weak, pitiable voice she told him. "But I don't want you staying here...helping me," she said defiantly.

"You don't have a choice. The sooner you accept my decision, the sooner you'll realize you might as well make the best of it."

She bit her lower lip and released it. Probably because she was weakened with pain, she sat very still. Finally, she nodded.

Maybe she wouldn't continue to be impossible. Maybe he was making headway toward his goal.

Or maybe after a night's sleep she'd rally and fight harder than ever.

He didn't care one way or the other. He wasn't leaving Daniel.

Or her.

Four

Luke sat on the couch as Daniel struggled to phonetically sound out the word *dog*.

How hard could it be to read that word?

Holding on to his patience, Luke caught his breath. Fortunately, Daniel got it and then read the rest of the sentence without any more problems.

Daniel had started kindergarten in the fall, and Caitlyn had told Luke the boy had to be helped with his reading every night. So Luke had volunteered.

Earlier, when she'd finally realized no amount of discussion would make Luke change his mind about staying, she'd taken a new tack. With a crafty smile, she'd said, "Well, if I'm stuck with you, we might as well find a way to make you useful."

"I'm sure I'll have plenty to do, fixing your finances."

"You know how it is on a ranch. There's always lots of hard, physical work to do, and with my ankle..."

"You win," he'd said with a smile.

She'd grabbed a pen and had dashed off a long list of chores. She'd probably chosen some of them, like mucking out stalls, because she remembered he'd thought they were unpleasant as hell.

Since he suspected the real purpose of her requests was to drive him away, he'd read the list and beamed as if in delight.

Except for the stall mucking, he'd charged through her tasks with an enthusiasm and competence that had irritated her to the extreme.

"Now, I have a list of my own, you know," he'd said when he'd finished. "On it are things you can do to please me. First thing is for you to cooperate. The second is that you need to let my chauffeur drive us both to your doctor and home again."

"You have so many stables to clean and horses to bathe, you have no time to waste on a trip to town with me," she'd said as he led her to the limo.

"Is grocery shopping in the number one position on your list or not, sweetheart? How can I do that if I don't go into town? I see right here that I'm supposed to buy feed. Where exactly is the feed store?" He'd got into the limo.

Sulkily she'd turned her back on him and stared out the window in gloomy silence, but he'd ignored her snit, using the quiet time in the limo to return several pressing international phone calls.

In the end, because he'd needed to make still more calls, including one to Teresa, he'd sent his driver to shop for groceries while he'd stayed with Caitlyn at her doctor's office.

The doctor diagnosed a sprained ankle. He'd put her in a boot, gave her crutches and told her to rest a couple of days before she started hobbling around outside.

"Do you have anybody who can help you, besides Manuel?" he'd asked. "I mean at night. In the house."

"Me," Luke had volunteered, slinging a possessive arm around her. "I'm staying at the house."

When she had flushed and tried to shrug free of his offending arm, the doctor cocked his eyebrows. "I see."

"It's not what you think," she'd muttered.

The doctor had smiled knowingly. "Then it's settled. Wonderful. You must rely on him for everything these first few days."

"Surely that's not necessary," she'd argued, trying to make light of her injury.

"Unfortunately, it is." The doctor had been adamant that if she was to get a full recovery, she needed to stay off her ankle for a good two weeks.

Smugly, Luke had taken charge. "You must be a good patient and do everything I say, sweetheart," he'd teased. "Doctor's orders."

The doctor had nodded conspiratorially while she'd silently fumed.

Luke had cooked their first shared supper—an

omelet and toast—and washed dishes and su-
pervised Daniel's bath. Then he'd played with
various action figures with the kid on the floor
of his room until she'd hobbled down the hall and
reminded them Daniel still needed to practice his
reading.

"Isn't it time for you to call it a day and forget
about issuing more commands?" Luke had asked
her after leading her to her bedroom. "You're
not getting rid of me, you know. The doctor put
me in charge. I run international corporations.
I think I can take care of one woman, one little
boy and a few horses and cows. Hell, cows feed
themselves."

Her brows had flown together at that. "You
know better than that."

"That I do," he'd said with a smile.

"I imagine in a day or two you'll be so bored
you'll be longing for London and your lavish lifestyle, not to mention your countess."

"That doesn't mean I'll leave Daniel. Then
there's Hassan. I promised him I'd help you."

Ignoring her pout, he'd poured her a glass of
water. When she'd dutifully swallowed her pain

pill, he said, "Good night. I'll say a prayer to whoever's listening that a night's sleep improves your attitude. You really are an incredibly difficult patient."

"Because of you! The only thing that could possibly improve my attitude is for you to—"

He'd leaned closer and touched her lips with a blunt fingertip. "Hush, before you say more mean things about the father of your son. You were in trouble long before I showed up. I'm here to help. So, good night. And that's final…unless you want me to tuck you in and kiss you good night." He'd said that only because she'd looked so cute frowning at him, that he'd forgotten they were at war.

Caught by surprise by his last comment, she'd glanced at his mouth and blushed most becomingly, her lips parting slightly, as if in invitation, before she'd caught herself.

Heat washed through him.

"Would you get out?"

"My pleasure," he'd whispered, smiling at her as he'd closed her door softly. "Sweet dreams."

Her eyes, deep and dark in her flushed face, had shot sparks at him.

Ten minutes later, Luke was still thinking about her brilliant, intelligent eyes and how they made her thin face even lovelier than the elegant Teresa's. Caitlyn's eyes warmed him, made him feel young and eager again, as he had when he'd been in love with her. Indeed, the memory of her brilliant eyes was still distracting him as Daniel labored through the story about a wise owl and an idiot mouse in need of a lesson.

Then the phone rang. Daniel, no doubt anxious for any excuse to stop reading, asked, "Can I quit now?"

"Yes. That was very good."

Not about to wait for Luke to change his mind, Daniel shot off the couch and ran down the hall to his room.

Damn, Luke thought, when the phone didn't ring again. Caitlyn, who was supposed to be asleep, must have answered the call. He was wondering what the caller wanted, when he heard a crash in her bedroom.

Afraid she'd gotten up and fallen, Luke rushed
down the hall and flung open her door.

Bathed in the golden glow of the bedside lamp,
she wore nothing but a pair of skimpy red lace
bikini panties. Leaning against one crutch, her
arms were outstretched as she bent to put on a red
bra. When the door banged open, she'd frozen,
staring up at him with huge dark eyes.

Erotic longing surged through him in a warm
tide. She blushed but made no move to cover
herself. The moment went on and on. Why did
she stand there in shock and let him devour the
sight of her lush figure?

Hell, why didn't he have the sense to look
away? But he couldn't. She was too beautiful.
His heart pounded violently, and his avid gaze
remained fixed on the voluptuous curves of her
hips and the globes of her firm, high breasts. He
couldn't have looked away had his life depended
on it.

Didn't she guess how powerfully she affected
him? Or did she? Was she doing this to seduce
him?

Feeling short of breath, he fought to control

himself. God help him, he wanted to pull her into his arms. He wanted to touch her more than he'd ever wanted to touch any woman.

He knew just how she'd feel if he were to lave her pink-tipped breasts with his tongue—as sweet and velvety and warmly luscious as the most luxurious dessert.

He wanted her, and what he felt wasn't casual. Her hold on his heart wasn't logical. In fact it was stupid. But it was a reality; and the reality irritated him.

"Didn't anyone teach you to knock?" she said in a furious whisper.

"Bubba never did put much stock in manners."

Hooking her bra, she grabbed her blouse and pulled it on.

"I heard something crash," he muttered. "I thought maybe you'd fallen…hurt yourself."

"I'm fine, as you can see. So you can go."

When she bent to pick up her jeans, he finally got a grip and turned his back on her. "What the hell do you think you're doing? Out of bed? You're hurt and on pain meds."

"I'm dressing. Manuel needs help. He's in the broodmare barn."

"You're not going out there!"

"I have to."

"No, I'll go."

"What good would you be?"

"Some things you don't forget."

"You could've fooled me when you spooked Ramblin' Man with your cell phone."

Her reminder about the phone rankled.

"I'm through dressing, so you can turn around now," she said.

He pivoted angrily. "I said I'll go. And that's the end of it. You're on crutches. Now get back in bed and stay there. Or I'll stay here, too—to watch over you." His voice softened dangerously on that last threat.

They gazed into each others' eyes, each wary. What was this force that drew them, bound them no matter how hard they both fought it?

Luke told himself to seize her crutches and go, but he couldn't.

"All right," she whispered. "You win."

She sank back down on the bed, causing the

mattress to groan and the sheets to rustle. Lying down again, she pulled the sheets up to her neck, but her eyes threw flames at him.

What was her game? If she truly wanted him gone, why had she stood there nearly naked, deliberately inviting his gaze?

She was the mother of his son and virtually alone out here. He felt responsible for her and the boy in ways he'd never felt responsible for anyone but himself. And whether she knew it or not, the one thing Luke had become very good at was living up to his responsibilities. He wasn't turning his back on his son or her.

Luke felt proud as he watched the mare and her newborn foal. At the end of the birth, the baby's legs had been tangled up and coming out wrong. Luke was glad the ordeal was over.

The foal had been gulping for every breath as they'd pulled him out. Luke had been so worried he'd wished he'd let Manuel call the vet, but by that point it had been too late. If they'd gone another few seconds without pulling out the colt, they would have lost him. Caitlyn had been right to doubt his abilities.

"Nice work," a woman's voice purred from behind him.

Luke turned and saw Caitlyn, looking almost as wobbly on her crutches as the foal did on his new legs. But her eyes were radiant as she studied him and the colt. Then she shook her dark hair back so that it slid over her shoulders like a heavy curtain of mussed silk.

"Didn't trust me, did you?" he mused.

"I'm afraid you're right. Couldn't sleep for imagining the worst," she whispered, "although I feel a bit groggy now."

"You shouldn't have come out here. You should be resting."

"It's hard to do what you should do sometimes, isn't it?" Her eyes burned him in the shadowy light. "At least you did one thing right today. But now you're a mess because of it—city slicker."

For the first time, he realized that the white shirt and jeans he'd put on before the afternoon's chores were covered in blood. "Right. Okay, show's over. I need a shower, and Manuel can finish up in here. You," he said to Caitlyn, "are going back to bed. Am I going to have to carry out my threat and move into your bedroom to keep you there?"

Again, her warm gaze locked with his in a way that made his stomach tighten with need.

"That won't be necessary," she whispered huskily, as he came out of the stall.

"Too bad."

"Don't start."

In spite of himself, he smiled. He felt proud of his work with the foal, and the approving light in her eyes made his heart leap. He was even hungrier to have her. Was she remembering how she'd stood in the lamplight, wearing nothing but her red panties, inviting his gaze?

He sure was.

And his desire for her was growing fiercer by the moment.

Five

Despite the pain medication she'd taken, Caitlyn drowsed fitfully for no more than an hour or two before bolting up from another all-too-familiar nightmare about her parents' car wreck. She always woke up just as the car veered off the bridge into the arroyo. Unlike Robert's death, which had occurred a mere month after theirs, their deaths had been unexpected.

After she caught her breath and quit sobbing, she heard what sounded like her door closing gently.

"Luke?" she cried softly.

He didn't answer.

Had he come to check on her? She heard a heavy footfall in the hall. Then his door opened and closed.

Why hadn't he answered her? Not that she wanted a repeat of earlier when he'd caught her dressing. Still, she felt vaguely disappointed that he'd ignored her when she'd called out to him.

Usually, when she woke up after one of her nightmares, she was all alone with Daniel. Sometimes knowing that her parents and Robert were gone and that the entire weight of Wild Horse Ranch's fate rested on her inadequate shoulders made her feel so desolate she wouldn't sleep for the rest of the night. In the mornings, she would face whatever challenge confronted her. But at night, she always felt vulnerable.

Growing up on the ranch, the place hadn't felt lonely. Her father and mother had been alive, and there'd been more hired hands. Of late, she hadn't been able to afford the skilled help she needed. When Daniel was at school, it was just her and Manuel.

For the first time since Luke's arrival she didn't mind so much that he was right down the hall, promising to help her sort out her affairs. She hadn't asked him here, and she hadn't wanted him. But his presence felt oddly comforting. He'd certainly made himself useful tonight in the barn, which was surprising considering his lavish life-style in London.

He'd taken charge of her recovery and had been unfailingly kind as well, not to mention resource-ful. He'd been unexpectedly good with Daniel, too, and the boy had taken to him. As she'd lis-tened to them read together, she'd realized Robert had rarely spent any time with the boy. Not that she'd blamed him. All Robert had ever promised Daniel was his name.

What if Luke really took a long-term interest in her son? That might be just what Daniel needed after losing Robert.... No, she couldn't let herself think about that. In all probability, Luke would tire of ranch life and the novelty of a son, as he'd tired of her so quickly all those years ago. And when he left again, he'd break her son's heart.

How could she prevent that? She risked havoc if she fought Luke. Hassan had sent him to help her, and now he'd found out about Daniel.

There were too many reasons why she had to work with him.

The pain in her ankle sharpened. Thinking to get her pain medication, she threw off the sheets and grabbed her crutches, but then she heard the sound of Luke's low voice on the porch. When he continued talking, curiosity got the best of her. Hobbling over to her window, she lifted the drape. She gasped at the sight of Luke leaning against a porch post with his phone pressed against his ear. He'd found the exact spot where the signal was best.

Who had he called after he'd left her? She strained to hear, but his deep voice was so low she couldn't catch a single word.

Pulling her robe over her thin nightgown, she laboriously swung herself down the hall. She opened the front door and soundlessly let herself outside.

"Hi, there," she called out, shivering in the chill breeze.

He whirled. Quickly he bit out a goodbye, saying words something to the effect of, "Gotta go, call you later." Then he slid his phone into his pocket.

"Talking to your girlfriend?" she asked, feeling a little put out at the thought of his beautiful countess. Not that his love life was any of her business, she reminded herself.

He neither confirmed nor denied who he had called as he walked toward her, which made her crankier. "It's 9:00 a.m. in London. I couldn't get a signal in the house, so I came outside."

"I'll take that as a yes."

"Think what you like."

He'd showered since she'd last seen him. Vaguely she remembered falling asleep to the sound of the water running while he'd sung a bawdy Western ballad off-key.

He smelled sexily of minty cologne and soap.

"Did you even go to bed?" she asked.

"Couldn't sleep. Jet lag. Problems with one of my newly acquired companies. I worked on my laptop awhile. What's your excuse?"

His white shirt was open at the throat, revealing tanned skin. His jeans molded to his muscular thighs. But it was the intensity of his dark, hooded gaze that challenged her and sent a trill of sensation up her spine. Suddenly it was very difficult to breathe.

You are the reason I can't sleep, she thought, praying he was unaware of her powerful reaction to him. How was she supposed to doze with such a virile hunk showering right down the hall, especially if he was the very man who triggered all the erotic memories and hot longings she'd fought for years?

How could he have left her back then, without even saying goodbye?

For a second longer his eyes remained as turbulent as her own wayward emotions and then he seemed to master some beast inside himself. Turning away, he picked up a glass from the railing, swirled it and drained it.

Did he have regrets, too?

With a sigh, she moistened her lip with her tongue.

He groaned and looked up at the sky. "Pretty night," he said. "I've missed stars." Then he turned and studied her. "Apparently, I've missed a lot of things I didn't know I missed." His heated gaze left her mouth and ran up and down her length, lingering in such a way as to stir her.

"My ankle hurt." She hoped her tone was matter-of-fact even though she felt a little breathless.

"Take more pain medication."

"I heard you out here. I was curious."

He leaned closer. "You know what they say? Curiosity leads little girls into big trouble. Especially if it involves a man."

She tossed her head back. "I can take care of myself."

"That being the case, I'd offer you a drink," he said smoothly, "but whiskey doesn't mix with those pain pills you're on."

He lifted a bottle of Robert's best whiskey off the floor and poured himself a second drink. "Hope you don't mind me raiding your liquor closet. I'll replace it."

"Drink all you want. It was Robert's. Just remember alcohol's not good for jet leg," she said rather primly. "You should be drinking water instead."

"Oh, really?" He chuckled, his green eyes flashing teasingly in the moonlight. "I remember a time when you weren't such a Goody Two-shoes. A time when you liked to live dangerously."

"I'm no Goody Two-shoes now," she snapped.

"And that is the gist of our problem." He stepped closer to her, so close she could smell the whiskey with the cologne, so close she could feel the heat of his body, fierce despite the cool night air.

Her nipples tightened against her thin cotton nightgown in reaction to him. Instead of backing away, fool that she was, she stood her ground, shivering a little, and not from the chill air.

"I know just how wild you are, sweetheart, and just how good you still taste. That's what's torturing the hell out of me. Being in the house with you, knowing you were right down the hall…was getting to me. So, I came out here. But being out here with the smell of grass and hay and dust in the air brings it all back—especially memories of you. Being here makes me feel almost like I never left. Why is that? What are you doing to me?"

"But you *did* leave. And you wouldn't have come back now of your own accord."

"You know why I left!"

She glared at him, remembering that her mother had said cash was missing from the truck when she'd explained why she'd had to let Luke go.

Still, he should have said goodbye.

"But I don't want to talk about all the bitter stuff. Not when this whiskey is so good. Not when you're standing out here looking so damn beautiful you make a grown man want to cry."

"As if you ever cry."

He laughed. "So why did *you* come out here on the porch? What do *you* want?" he demanded. "Are you chasing me, girl, like you used to? Because this time I don't aim to run."

"Of course not!" When he laughed again, she caught her lower lip in her teeth and stared at him uncertainly. Was he right? Had she been chasing him? Just a little?

No! But he did look uncompromisingly masculine and devastatingly attractive.

"I'd better go back inside," she whispered raggedly.

"Too late, sweetheart. You should have thought about that before you came out here to tempt me."

"I did not come out here for that reason!"

"I think you did. And I think I know exactly what you want. I'll give it to you, sweetheart, anytime. Just say the word."

"Not in this lifetime."

"Really?" He laughed again. "This is only our first night. We're both exhausted, and you're injured. Even so, neither of us can sleep because we know what we want. Because we know how good it would be."

Afraid of him, and the feelings and memories he aroused, she turned to go, but he seized her by the arm. His hands gripped her waist, snugging her against his long, lean body. At such close range she could see the curve of his thick black lashes and the tiny lines fanning beneath his glittering eyes. His sensual mouth was full and much too kissable.

He frowned down at her, staring at her in a fierce way that made her blood fire and her willpower dissolve.

"You shouldn't have come back," she said. "Hassan should have sent someone else."

"If it weren't for Daniel, I'd agree. But we have

a son, and Hassan suspected Daniel was mine right from the first."

"How do you know that?"

"He told me. On the phone. Right after I saw Daniel. So I came back. And discovered we still have this…"

"This…this what?" A wild, tender sweetness filled her. For a second she was in the past, when she was in love with him. Back then he'd made it easy to believe that his feelings for her had run as deep as hers for him.

She wanted him to kiss her again, to feel his tongue in her mouth. She wanted his large hands on her body, their fingertips blistering her through her thin nightgown.

"Don't pretend you don't feel it, too. This insane, completely self-destructive need," he growled, lowering his mouth to the throbbing hollow of her throat where her pulse beat madly. "I thought it was dead. I willed it to be dead. But it's stronger than ever."

Hissing in a breath, she swallowed tightly as his warm lips devoured her neck, nibbling her soft flesh, flooding her body with hot melting sensations.

"Let me go! You're just a long way from home and feeling horny."

His smile was grim. "I wish to hell that was all this was. I wish to hell…"

Her heart fluttered at the desperate passion in his tone. Did he feel more?

He plunged his fingers into her hair. "I used to love your hair. I loved the way you smelled—like Texas wildflowers in the spring. Nothing's changed. You smell just as sweet, and you're just as soft—underneath your thorny exterior. You're sexier than ever, and I still want you. I told myself for years I hated you. Maybe I do. But right now I want you so much I don't care how the hell you used me."

She wanted his mouth on her lips, wanted to lie under him, but the savage anger in his passion-drugged voice brought her up short.

He had some nerve to accuse *her* of using *him*. She was not about to take such abuse from a man who'd stolen money from her parents, a man whose abandonment had nearly destroyed her.

What had she ever done to him except adore him? Nothing. He was to blame for everything that had gone wrong between them. He'd taken everything she'd given and had let her parents down, as well. Then he'd trashed the most beautiful moment in her life by walking out on her without even a goodbye or an explanation.

With a final lust-filled glance at his sensual mouth, she placed her hand against Luke's hard-muscled chest and pushed with all her strength.

"You're right. I shouldn't have come out here. I'm tired. My ankle hurts. I need my pain meds. And the last thing I need is you, a skilled seducer of women, pressing yourself on me."

"What?" With eyes that were dazed with desire, he stared at her hard, trying to focus. Finally, the thin set of her lips and slitted gaze must have convinced him she meant what she said. He sucked in a hard breath and loosened his grip.

"Okay. I forgot your low opinion of me when it comes to women." His voice was curt. "But for future reference, don't go following me around in the middle of the night now that you know what I want. I've made myself plain, so I'll think you're bloody well asking for it."

"Well, I won't be!" she lied. "This is my house and I'm used to having the run of it! I won't be told what to do or where to go in my own home!" She wanted to snap out more sharp, stinging lines, but she was too upset—and too needy for the same things he'd said he wanted. She didn't want to leave him, but she had to.

Her knees felt weak, and her hands were shaking. No telling what despicable thing she might still be capable of doing with him if she didn't put some distance between them. Besides, he had the look of a man who was barely holding himself in check.

"Whether you like it or not, you're not living out here alone anymore," he growled. "I'm a man with a man's inclinations."

"I got it the first time," she said in a low tone that sounded much calmer. But she wasn't calm. She was furious. "I don't like you giving orders in my house."

"Your house? It won't be for long—unless you

work with me! You and I have to figure out a way to rein in expenses, sell acreage or…"

"I don't want to talk about money tonight."

"You're right. It's premature."

Notching her chin up proudly, she turned to go. Then, as quickly as she could while hampered by her crutches and the knowledge that his gaze burned her backside, she walked to the front door. Once inside she made her way down the hall, stopping to check on Daniel before returning to her own room.

Long after she took more pain meds, she lay in bed feeling hot and needy. Her skin burned with the memory of him watching her dress and the blistering warmth she'd felt when he'd stared at her with such longing. Even now, some wayward part of her reveled in how urgently he'd clasped her to him on the porch.

Part of her wanted to walk down the hall to his room, slide into his bed and wait for him to come inside so she could melt against his body and beg him to take her. She wanted him to kiss her endlessly. She wanted him inside her. She wanted sex, fast and hard, the kind of sex she hadn't had since he'd left. Not that she'd had *any* sex—period. Maybe if she had him again, she would wake up free of his dark spell once and for all.

But she wasn't a man. She wasn't as comfortable owning her true sexual feelings and needs as he obviously was. She was overly emotional about sex with Luke and had most likely romanticized it.

When he'd made love to her in the barn that long-ago evening, he'd been infinitely gentle. He'd kissed her, held her, took the time to pleasure her, said sweet things that had made her feel special.

"I've never been with a virgin before. I want it to be perfect for you," he'd said in an awed tone, pulling her close.

And it had been. Maybe because she'd been so madly in love with him, and he'd seemed equally in love.

The second time he'd made love to her, he'd been driven. Yet nothing had ever made her feel so adored and complete as his shattering climax.

Now, an hour or so after leaving the porch, she

was still awake, when she finally heard him come back inside.

Holding her breath, she listened as he shot the bolt. Then she counted his footsteps as he walked down the hall to his room. She heard him come out and go into the hall bathroom and take another long shower.

A cold one, to quell his desire? Or a steamy one to relax him?

How could even the sound of the tap arouse her, making her imagine him tall and naked? But it did. She felt wet and oh so achingly hot. Then he shut off the water, and that was worse. She imagined him warm and solid, his hard body wrapped in a white towel that would be so easy to remove, if only she had the nerve to admit all the things he'd accused her of.

Fisting her sheets, she told herself she had to be strong.

After his bedroom door closed a second time, she couldn't stop thinking about him lying in his bed alone. She relaxed her hands, but her heart continued to race. More than anything, she wanted to go to him.

She threw off the sheets and sat up. Tearing off her nightgown, she lay down again and stretched out in the dark. With fingertips that trembled she began to touch herself, imagining Luke's hands on her body, bestowing all the forbidden caresses she craved.

Six

The next morning when Caitlyn woke up an hour later than usual, she was shivering because she was nude and her covers had fallen off. Leaning forward, she pulled the sheets and blankets over her and lay nestled in a plump pile of feather pillows. She was glad she didn't have to do chores or get Daniel off to school. Feeling groggy and disoriented from her injuries and the pain medication, she lay there for some time, savoring the pleasant sensation of warmth and quiet in her semidarkened bedroom. How nice it was that Luke was here to shoulder a few of her responsibilities.

With a sigh, she remembered dreaming of Luke making love to her. For a moment or two she savored those dreams, but as she grew more alert, she became unhappily aware that he was the last man she should be fantasizing about. He'd abandoned her. He was a billionaire with a beautiful countess for a girlfriend. No way could he ever be seriously interested in someone like her again. Not that she would want him to be. No—most definitely not. He was only here for Hassan and Daniel.

Annoyed now, she sat up straighter and switched on the light. Immediately her gaze fell to the silky folds of her peach nightgown, which lay neatly on top of her bedside table. On top of her gown was a slip of paper, which she greedily seized.

It was a note from Luke saying he'd fed Daniel and had gone down to the main road with him to wait until the school bus came. She wadded up the note and then unwadded it and reread the boldly flowing black script.

Luke had come in here and seen her naked!

As she imagined him standing over her, she

felt a mixture of embarrassing emotions—desire, shame, tenderness. She imagined his gaze feasting on the sight of her body as she lay nude. She really should hate this almost pleasurable reaction to what was really an uncalled-for invasion of her privacy. What had he thought when he'd found her twisted nightgown on the floor and her covers thrown off?

He certainly hadn't seized the opportunity to awaken her and take advantage. No, instead he'd made himself useful by getting Daniel fed and off to school. In spite of herself, she was impressed that a shallow, wealthy bachelor would have known what to do without waking her and asking for her expert advice.

The thought of him caring enough to put himself out, even that little bit, for their son—and for her—touched her heart in ways that it shouldn't.

It doesn't mean anything. Daniel's a novelty to him right now. And he did it for his son, not to please me.

She was *not* falling under his spell again! He'd betrayed her family's trust and left as if she'd meant nothing.

She got up and dressed. Her routine took much longer than usual—the crutches made every step slower, and she normally didn't waste time on makeup or finding her most flattering pair of jeans.

When she finally reached the kitchen in jeans so tight she wanted to scream, she found Luke's rinsed cup in the sink along with a fresh pot of coffee.

Breathless from dragging herself around, she poured herself a steaming cup and sat down at the table. She already ached under her arms from the crutches. On a normal morning she would have been up and out hours ago. She'd taken her good health for granted. Now that she was helpless and dependent on Luke, not to mention so attracted to him she was torturing herself by wearing skin-tight jeans, she felt confused and out of sorts.

She wanted him gone before he knew his full power over her, but hampered by her ankle, she couldn't go about her usual chores without him. Horses needed to be fed, watered, exercised, clocked, bred, inoculated and prepared for shipping. Someone had to deal with drivers, who needed documents signed. Stalls had to be cleaned.

If only she had a larger staff, she could avoid Luke. But with Daniel away at school, and Manuel being her only full-time employee, she would have to spend a lot of time with her ex-lover. Luke had dismissed his driver, so he'd be driving her to town for a follow-up with the doctor and the rescheduled appointment with her accountant.

So much togetherness was not good. She seemed to be becoming obsessed with the man. But what could she do other than endure him until she was better?

The most hateful question of all: what would she have done without him?

Lost in a circle of worries, she heard the unfamiliar ringtone of a phone coming from the living room. Thinking the call might be important, she slid her crutches under her aching armpits and hobbled toward Luke's phone.

A name stood out in bold black on the screen: Teresa Wellsley.

Caitlyn bit her lip. No matter how dependent on him she was, she had to remember Luke had a life that included a beautiful countess named Teresa. He might desire Caitlyn, but that was probably because she was the only woman available at the moment.

She couldn't let herself forget about Teresa. Not for a minute.

"So when did they die?" Luke asked softly from behind her.

A shiver of excitement coursed through her at the nearness of Luke's soft voice. All morning she'd fought to remain emotionally aloof, but that was proving difficult. He was being so nice.

She hadn't wanted him to accompany her on this errand. Using a garden hose, Caitlyn splashed water on the green lawn and flowers surrounding her parents' immaculately kept graves, which were located in the cowboy cemetery half a mile from the ranch house.

"Nearly a year ago. In a car wreck. There was a violent thunderstorm. Mother was driving. You know how she always had to be in charge."

When he nodded grimly, she remembered that her mother had never liked him. Her mother had even seemed to relish firing him for stealing, because she'd been proven right.

"Nobody knows what happened. Maybe she was avoiding an animal. Their car skidded off that bridge just outside of town."

"Into the arroyo?" His low, sympathetic tone made her heart catch.

She nodded. "The car rolled and caught fire. The sheriff said they died instantly."

"I liked your father. Before Hassan, he was the only man who saw the good in me."

Caitlyn appreciated the fact that he admired her father and didn't run her mother down. He could have held a grudge, despite his own guilt. Her mother had never been one to keep her opinions to herself, and her opinion of Luke, from the first, had been that her husband never should have hired Bubba Kilgore's trashy son. She'd never let her father forget how Luke had betrayed him by taking the much-needed cash from the truck.

"Dad liked you a lot, too," Caitlyn said, suddenly recalling that her father had been an excellent judge of character while her mother had always been more impressed by wealth and show. As Bubba's boy, Luke had had nothing to recommend him to her mother back then. After she'd fired him, her mother had been quick to point out it was a blessing in disguise in that it freed Caitlyn to marry Robert.

"Maybe your mother would have liked me better if you hadn't chased me so boldly."

It probably wouldn't have mattered. Her mother had wanted Caitlyn to end up with Robert Wakefield because his daddy owned Wild Horse Ranch at the time. But there were hard truths about Robert that might have made her mother think differently. She'd definitely have a change of opinion about Luke, if she could see him now. What was a little missing cash compared to an income in the billions?

"I enjoyed defying my mother by flirting with you. I couldn't stand the way she always tried to run my life, even after I was an adult, but I miss her. I miss both of them. I felt so alone after their accident, which happened a few weeks before

Robert died. Now that they are all gone, I have no one I can talk to."

Was that why she was talking to Luke as if they were friends? Was that why her resistance to him was dissolving so quickly?

"I felt all alone after my mother died, too," he said. "Dad was so far gone. It was because of your father that I began to see a way out."

She wanted to ask why he'd taken the money when he could have asked for a loan, but she didn't.

"In a way, I owe your dad as much as I owe Hassan. Which means I owe his daughter, as well."

"You owe me nothing! Daddy always said you were an incredible worker."

"It's the trait that made Hassan take a chance on me. Money can be very destructive in the wrong hands. For a man with no self-discipline, no goals, there are many temptations. Hassan wouldn't have backed me had I lacked the determination to withstand corruption."

Those weren't the words of a thief. Was he speaking the truth? She hadn't asked him about the money or why he'd left. She'd believed her mother.

Did she have a false opinion of him and his life in London? Was he really a wealthy man who used his money to attract and then discard beautiful women? He didn't act like he was. From the moment he'd found out about Daniel, he'd put his son first. Not only that, he'd gone out of his way to help her. He'd been sent here to work on her finances, but he'd done so much more.

No! She would be a fool to reverse her poor opinion of him so easily. He'd left her! Her mother had sworn he'd stolen money. He'd left *Daniel.* Why should she give him the benefit of the doubt just because he was so sexy, just because he listened and paid attention?

Luke's silence made her nervous.

Caitlyn hated suspense. As a child she'd hated counting the days until Christmas. When her parents had taken her on trips, she'd pestered them every five minutes with, "Are we there yet?"

This was more suspense than she could handle. It was late in the afternoon of their first full day together. He'd arrived only yesterday, but it seemed longer.

Rosy sunlight slanted across the pasture as she stood outside her barn watching Luke shave Angel's whiskers with an electric razor. What she wanted was for him to give her some clue as to his plans for her ranch's future.

Besides taking her to the doctor and the accountant, he'd spent most of the day studying her operation, yet he hadn't said anything. Now, his attention was maddeningly focused on her big darlings, who were flirting with him like a pair of shameless hussies. He was laughing as Lilly inserted her nose between his hand and Angel's head.

"Lilly wants her turn," he said. "I think she's jealous."

"Indeed."

Luke smiled. "Maybe she isn't the only one."

"Lilly's superaffectionate with everybody!" It rankled that her big babies had taken such a fancy to Luke and were vying for his attention while ignoring her. But, he'd always been as good with horses as he was with women.

He turned the razor back on. When he finished with Lilly, he stroked both horses and gave them carrots to munch. They neighed and nudged his shirt pocket with their noses.

"Like women, they love attention and presents," he said. "I'm not above carrying around a few carrots to win their favor."

As he stroked Lilly, she felt like she would burst if he didn't tell her what he thought.

After getting Daniel off to school and taking her to her parents' graves, he'd driven her into town to see the doctor and Bruce, her accountant. The three of them had gone over the books, and during a quick business lunch Luke had asked Bruce lots of probing questions. Although Luke had taken a few notes, he'd said little, thus revealing none of his thoughts on the subject.

Bruce's grim listing of the bare facts and his obvious relief that a man as successful as Luke was here to help had unsettled her stomach so much she'd left most of her sandwich on her plate. She didn't like being dependent on anyone, much less Luke Kilgore. But what choice did she have?

Luke had insisted they have a conference call

with Al Johnson, a ranch manager in between jobs, a man with numerous successes in turning around ranching operations like hers.

"But I can't afford a manager, and I don't want some stranger telling me what to do," she'd said.

Upon returning to the ranch, Luke had insisted she rest, while he'd driven her ATV to the various barns and paddocks and pastures, inspecting everything. When he'd returned, he'd still offered nothing.

She couldn't take his silence anymore!

"Okay! So, you've spent the whole day thinking about Wild Horse Ranch. Did you come up with a financial solution or not?"

"Don't worry. These things take time," he murmured, not looking at her as he stroked Lilly's muzzle. "You need to concentrate on healing."

She heaved in a breath. Under different circumstances, she might have enjoyed hanging out with him and her horses, since he was being so pleasant. But not today. Not when she wanted to know what he was thinking.

"Surely you could give me some hint as to what you think, what you'll tell Hassan. What was his attitude when you last talked to him? Is he worried enough to shut me down?"

"Hassan could afford to bankroll you indefinitely. So could I, for that matter."

"You? Why would I want that? I want Wild Horse Ranch to be a solid business."

"There's always more than one way to skin a cat," he said. "The ranching part of your operation is in the black. It's the horse business that's jeopardizing everything."

As if she didn't already know that. The horses were her passion.

"Like Al said over the phone, you need to raise capital and lower your debt. You could sell some of your bloodstock. I wrote down my thoughts on what I'd sell if I took that route. I called Al back and we discussed—"

"No. I've been building my breeding stock for years."

"Building too fast, it would seem. With horses that haven't always panned out."

"I had a run of bad luck."

"A run you couldn't afford. Surely you understand that you can't keep borrowing without jeopardizing the entire ranch—again. It wasn't so long ago that your father lost it to the bank during that terrible drought. Remember? When I lived here, your father had just moved your family back to the ranch, but he was leasing it from the Wakefields."

"Of course I remember! Who could forget such a thing?"

"Any rich boyfriends like Wakefield waiting in the wings to save you this time?" There was an odd predatory glint in his eyes.

"Don't joke about something like that."

His expression hardened. He didn't look like he was joking. "So, you're not dating anyone seriously?" he asked in a lower tone.

A little gasp escaped her throat. "That is none of your business!"

"Well, are you?"

"No!" she snapped before she had time to think of a clever lie. "And the only reason I'd ever marry again is for love!"

"I wonder—were your motivations equally noble when you married Wakefield?"

She almost choked. "Of course they were!" she

sputtered indignantly. "I loved Robert! We grew up together!"

"How reassuring. But if you did marry for money, there's no shame in it. How do you think the aristocratic families in England have kept their estates intact for hundreds of years?"

"How would I know?"

"All too often, marrying well is the only practical thing to do."

Was that why he considered his countess so perfect? Or maybe that was why the countess considered *him* so perfect.

Caitlyn wasn't about to admit she'd learned her lesson about marrying for the wrong reasons, so she bit her tongue and gloomily watched him stroke Lilly with his long, tanned fingers.

"I don't care about aristocratic families in your precious England," she said.

"Well, if you don't like the idea of marrying for money, maybe you could take in a rich partner."

"Someone with a big ego like yours, who'd want to call all the shots?"

"Okay. You could syndicate some of your mares."

"That would mean even more male egos to deal with."

"You could lease Wild Horse Ranch and work here on a salary."

"And lose all control? No! I don't like any of your so-called solutions."

"I could hire Al Johnson to run the place for a while. He could make the brutal cuts that are necessary, get things running smoothly and then teach you how—"

"No! I was afraid of that...."

"Look, you can't keep doing what you're doing. Why don't you sleep on these ideas, and we'll talk again tomorrow morning. There's nothing like a good night's sleep to make one more amenable to practicalities."

"I'm not changing my mind."

"All right, sweetheart, if you're sure—I do have another solution."

"What?"

"Since you've been so negative about all my other suggestions, I think I'll keep it to myself for now."

"It's my life and my ranch you're playing God with. Just tell me!"

"When I'm ready. Remember, you played God with my son for five years."

She heaved in a breath. His response infuriated her, but he did have a point about Daniel. Then something hot and dark flashed in his eyes, causing her to shiver.

"What?" she whispered.

His gaze fell to her lips and then lower, raking over her figure in the skin-tight jeans that she'd worn just to provoke him.

Heat consumed her. Her skin felt raw. Hating the wild flare of her rampaging emotions, she wished she'd worn something baggy. She was a fool to have dressed to entice him, when his glance left her breathless and made her sizzle.

"Sorry to upset you," he said dryly. "That's not my intention."

"I wish I could believe you." She frowned at him. "I don't like waiting," she whispered. "That's all."

His hungry gaze slid over her a second time.

"What could possibly be more enjoyable than... anticipation?"

"Lots of things...when it comes to dealing with you."

He laughed.

Suddenly, because of his nearness, she was restless.

When she stamped her boot, his laughter deepened into something bolder. "Enjoy," he whispered in a low, seductive voice before turning and leading her big darlings to their stalls.

Knotting her hands around her crutches, she watched him disappear with her horses into the shadowy barn.

Being in Luke's power was unendurable. How could he force her to consider all those unpleasant business options while keeping her in the dark about his true intentions? She had no doubt that his final solution would be worse than anything he'd mentioned so far. Otherwise he would simply tell her. If he was any other man, she'd think he was afraid.

She wanted to call him a coward. She wanted

to kick him. But as long as he had financial control over Wild Horse Ranch, she had to restrain herself and put up with him.

Seven

A red sun stained the twisting branches of the live oaks as Luke and Daniel stirred the coals of their fire. Caitlyn stood apart from them, feeling increasingly uneasy as she watched the blaze.

The copse had once been his private refuge, but after she'd followed him here, it had become their special meeting place. He'd even carved their names in the center of a heart on a tree trunk.

She didn't like it one bit that he'd picked this particular oak motte for their supper tonight. It stirred way too many unwanted memories.

Earlier she'd pleaded with him. "Why can't we just eat a quick meal in the house?"

"Because a picnic in the oak motte would be much more fun."

"Not for me. Besides, you're not here for fun. You're here to solve my problems. And then leave."

His quick, knowing glance had reminded her that she had no clue as to his true intentions.

"I meant more fun for Daniel," he'd said as he'd thrown hamburger buns, bananas, marshmallows and a pair of rusty tongs into a bag.

"Yes! I want to go, Mom!"

When Daniel had smiled at her, there had been no way for her to argue further.

And Daniel was having the time of his life. Luke had let him build the fire. Now, as he stirred the flames a bit too aggressively with a long stick, he sent brilliant sparks popping into the dry leaves.

"Why can't we cook the marshmallows now?" he demanded, as more sparks flew.

Luke jumped over the ring of rocks surrounding the fire and stamped on the burning leaves with his boots. "After supper," Luke replied for the third time without the slightest trace of annoyance.

In spite of her misgivings, Caitlyn smiled. Luke, who'd waited at the bus stop for Daniel to return from school, was extremely patient and attentive with the boy in a way that Robert never had been. Daniel's noise, constant demands and clutter had driven Robert crazy, especially after he'd become ill.

"Mom never likes me to come here," Daniel said.

"As if that's ever stopped you," Caitlyn said. "This copse is your favorite hiding place, isn't it?"

"Because I know you won't follow me here."

For her, the shady grove was haunted by her memories. Here, Luke had imprisoned her against a tree trunk with his hands and kissed her until her toes had curled.

"It used to be my favorite place on the ranch, too," Luke said, his gleaming eyes meeting hers in a challenge. "Some of my fondest memories happened in this oak motte." He stared at Caitlyn. "I even carved my name on a tree to stake my claim on something precious that once belonged to me."

She gasped. "That tree was cut down a long time ago!"

"You've been here before, Luke?" Daniel whispered.

"I used to work for your grandfather," he said, releasing her from his gaze to look at Daniel.

"For Paw Paw? You did? Wow! When was that?"

"A long, long time ago."

"How come Mom didn't tell me? Mom?"

When Luke's sardonic gaze flew to hers along with Daniel's searching one, her heart skittered wildly. "You'd have to ask her," he said.

"Mom just told me you were a rich guy who buys horses."

"Well, she was right…as far as it goes. But your mom and I, we're old friends."

"Not anymore," she inserted quickly. "That was another lifetime."

Strange, but suddenly it felt like yesterday. The past seemed all too vivid beneath the sheltering shade of these familiar trees.

"But once—we were very good friends," Luke insisted. "The best friends ever."

When she shot him a warning glance, Daniel looked from her to Luke in confusion.

"Are y'all keeping a secret or something?"

Her heart thudded violently.

"We were friends—before she married your father," Luke added.

"But I didn't know Luke was coming here yesterday," she blurted out. "He just showed up out of the blue."

"Well, I'm glad he did. And I'm glad he's going to help us," Daniel said, looking both innocent and pleased. "'Cause now you won't have anything to worry about anymore. Luke's great at just about everything, isn't he, Mom?"

If only she were still as innocent as her son and could believe in Luke's inherent goodness. Once, she'd seen Luke as her very own hero cowboy, riding in to save the day. She hadn't believed him capable of the low things her mother had warned her about and later accused him of.

"He's Bubba's son," her mother had said. "Oh, he's handsome, I'll give you that, girl. But he can't be faithful, and he'll prove what he is soon enough."

Caitlyn, who'd felt the sting of his betrayal on all levels and knew the pain of innocence lost, felt increasingly threatened by him, both personally and financially.

How would he use his power over her and her son?

It didn't matter that Caitlyn knew what Luke was capable of. Her sexy house guest had her thinking about him day and night.

Luke, with his silky black hair. Luke, with his powerful shoulders and lean body. Luke, with the devil's own grin.

Last night had been particularly sleepless. Thus, on the third morning of his stay, as she watched his tanned hand stab a thick slab of ham in the too-intimate confines of her tiny kitchen, she felt too near her breaking point. Slamming her coffee cup down on the table, she leaned toward him.

When he tensed and jumped back from his eggs, she smiled triumphantly. Maybe she wasn't the only one on edge.

For the last two nights she'd barely slept. Not that she'd stripped off her nightgown again or touched herself—even though she'd wanted to. No, instead, she'd lain awake for hours, listening to every creak of the house, thinking about Luke lying in his bed down the hall. She'd ached for him.

"You've been here two full days."

"Don't forget the nights," he murmured in a low tone.

At the mention of those nights, which she'd deliberately avoided saying anything about, warm color crawled up her neck.

"I want to get this over with! So what's your mysterious solution to my problem?" she demanded. "What is it? You have to tell me!"

He set his fork on his plate with a clatter and stood up. "Do I, now?"

Was he as nervous around her as she was around him? Did he feel ensnared by the sensual tension that had her emotions so tangled? She might think he was simply afraid to answer her question, but she knew Luke wasn't afraid of anything.

After placing his dishes in the sink, his lean, broad-shouldered back was to her. He called down the hall to remind Daniel it was time for them to wait for the school bus.

Refusing to be ignored in such a high-handed manner in her own home, she shot out of her chair, only to wince when her ankle touched the floor. Blinking back tears and taking a quick breath to clear the pain, she carefully hobbled to the sink. Leaning on one crutch, she said, "Surely you have things to do in London."

"Many things."

"Teresa being one of them?"

He turned. The lean, bronzed face that had haunted her dreams was taut with mockery. "For someone who claims she is utterly indifferent, you do take an inordinate interest in my love life. I can't help but wonder why."

That he saw through her so easily galled. "Why can't you just cut to the chase, so we can get this over with and go on with our lives?" she snapped.

"Since I know about Daniel, 'going on with our lives' is not possible any longer." He stared down at her, studying her too intently through his long, sooty lashes. "Is that what you really want—me gone and out of your life?"

"Of course. But I can't help but wonder what my life here will be like if you change the way the ranch is run. I heard you talking to Al Johnson again yesterday. Why did you call him? Is he coming here? In what capacity? Why? What are you planning? The suspense is killing me."

"I can see that, and I'm sorry."

"Tell me what you plan to do."

"All in good time," he repeated. "Much as I enjoy your company and the possibility of a spirited argument, we don't want Daniel to be late to school, do we?"

Mutely, she shook her head. Without another word on the subject, he turned and stomped down the hall to hurry their son along—a necessary chore, since Daniel was so easily distracted. He was probably playing with an action figure instead of putting on his shoes at this very moment.

Still, she wanted to run or, rather, hobble after Luke and badger him into telling her. But she knew him well enough to realize she would humiliate herself to no purpose. No doubt her curiosity amused him. The wiser course was to wait him out. Otherwise, he'd simply dig in his heels and put off telling her for even longer.

Thus, several more days passed without him referring to the matter at hand and with her biting her tongue to keep from drilling him. Even after she threw away her crutches and was able to resume her full routine, never once did he allude to his mysterious solution other than to ask if she'd reconsidered any of his other options.

When she'd said no, he'd seemed almost content to settle down to ranch life. When he wasn't making international calls or working on his laptop, he made himself useful by helping with Daniel and assisting Manuel with the heavier work. He didn't complain, either.

But with the passing of more days and nights— interminable, sleepless nights—she felt the raw, too-intimate, highly charged sensual cravings between them build.

Last night when he'd come out of the hall bathroom, shirtless, he'd nearly bumped into her. She'd caught her breath and barely managed the willpower to skitter down the hall into her own room and bolt the door.

This morning when she'd caught a glimpse of him through the cracked bathroom door as he'd shaved, his dark head cocked to one side and his white shirt unbuttoned, the mere sight of so much tanned muscle had sent tingles through every nerve in her body. She'd known the sensual joy of his body. The man lured her, as only the drug of choice can lure an addict who knows its pleasure full well and has been forced to do without for too long.

That evening after supper, she was grumpy as she faced still another sleepless night brooding over a man she did not *want* to want. He'd had another conversation with Al Johnson without telling her what they'd talked about. She wanted to know what he was up to, but some crisis had erupted in London. For more than an hour, he'd been holed up in her dining room behind closed doors, engaged in a tense overseas conference call with several of his top London executives.

She didn't want to eavesdrop, but his deep, hard voice carried. Apparently, the employees at

Kommstarr, his most recently acquired company, didn't like the massive changes he was instigating. Never had he sounded more ruthless than he did when he insisted his executives slash jobs and budgets and make lists of assets to be sold.

These were people's lives he was dealing with! She couldn't help but wonder what chance her horse farm had. Would he coldly demand that she sell her darlings? After all, they were mere horses.

He had to think his solution would upset her, or he'd tell her what it was. How could she lie awake longing for such a tough, arrogant brute? Maybe she was better off not knowing what he intended for Wild Horse Ranch.

She had to tune out his impending decision or she would go crazy dwelling on all the scenarios she could dream up. Summoning her willpower, she marched to Daniel's room, thinking she'd read her son a chapter of *Harry Potter,* only to find her precious darling curled up on his bed, with his blanket pulled up to his chin. She didn't like the way his green eyes burned in his thin, flushed face.

"Mommy, I'm c-cold," he said through teeth that chattered.

"Honey! What's the matter?" When she leaned down and felt him, his forehead was hot. "We'd better take your temperature," she said before rushing to the bathroom to find the thermometer.

Luke was closing his phone and stepping out of the dining room when she dashed back into Daniel's room with the thermometer.

"What's wrong?"

"I think Daniel's got a fever."

Luke stood over her as she took Daniel's temperature.

"He's got a fever. I'll give him a cool bath and some medicine," she said. "If he's not better in the morning, we'll call Dr. Williams."

After bathing him, she gave Daniel a hug and put him to bed early with a great many toys to comfort him. Later, as she lay awake in her bed, her thoughts were on Daniel rather than on Luke's mysterious solution. Still, she was aware of Luke getting up during the night to check on Daniel.

Around midnight, when she hadn't heard Luke in a while, she decided to check on Daniel herself. But when she tiptoed to his room, Daniel's door opened and Luke stepped out into the hall wearing only his black pajama bottoms.

As soon as she saw him, the hair on her nape pricked with sensual awareness. "How is he?" she whispered, pulling the edges of her thin robe together with shaking fingertips.

"His fever broke. He's fine—now."

"Is he?" She attempted to make her voice casual as she slipped past him and went inside to make sure. Their bodies brushed, and the heat of his skin set off jitters at all her pleasure points.

After sliding her palm across her son's cool forehead, she adjusted his blankets and his favorite stuffed animals. Immensely reassured that he would probably be perfectly well by morning, she came back out into the hall, clutching a stuffed brown bear, only to start when Luke called her name from the dark.

She turned. He stood beside their son's open door, his feet planted wide apart.

Their gazes met. At the sight of all that muscle and the black hair on his wide chest, she clenched the bear protectively to her breasts.

"You're right," she said in a breathy voice. "He's fine. Just had to make sure."

Luke's fine bone structure looked even tauter than usual in the dimly lit hall. What was it about the dark that made her blood run wilder?

Despite the danger Luke posed, she was terribly glad she wasn't on the ranch alone with a sick child. Luke cared about Daniel, as she did. He seemed to feel the same profound responsibility, which amazed her since he'd known his son for only a few days. But because he did feel so strongly about Daniel, she felt linked to him by more than mere desire.

Why, fool that she was, she was beginning to believe in him again, as she had when she'd been in love with him. It seemed impossible that such a man would rob an employer he'd respected and abandon a woman he'd loved. He didn't seem capable of such unsavory behavior now, and she wondered if he ever had been.

Suddenly, as she continued to stare at him hungrily, she remembered Luke's warning that first night when she'd followed him out to the porch.

So, what was she doing—standing in the hall, ogling him?

It was always a mistake to mix business with pleasure. The fate of Wild Horse Ranch was in his hands. If for no other reason, she should fight her attraction.

If she didn't want to send the wrong message to this man who held such power over her, she should say a curt good-night and march into her bedroom and shut the door.

Instead, she continued to stare at him, her heart pounding and her breath fluttering.

When he took a step toward her, an electric shock went through her. Even then, she remained where she was, shivering from the thrill of what might happen next. He took another soundless, heart-thudding step. And then another. And another.

"Caitlyn?" The bold challenge in his emerald eyes set off a pulsing excitement that sizzled through her even before he reached out to touch her.

"Luke?" Torn, she backed away from him.

"Come to me," he whispered thickly. "Just let me hold you."

She should run. She knew that. His past betrayal stood between them. The role he intended to play in Daniel's life was still uncertain. He had the beautiful, perfect Teresa waiting for him in London. Teresa, the countess who probably had soft hands and a softer life. But right now, London and Hassan and all their unresolved issues seemed so far away.

Feeling strange and excited, Caitlyn took a tremulous step toward him, and then another, until she stood close enough to touch him. She trembled with the need to slide her hands over his body. Still, she hesitated.

"Luke," she breathed.

He touched her first, causing her to shudder. Wasting no more time, he gently framed her face with his blunt fingers and plundered her mouth in a long, hard kiss. His tongue plunged inside, taking possession of her.

Her heartbeat quickened. Rising on her tiptoes, she kissed him back for all she was worth.

A fierce laugh erupted from his throat as he

caught her closer and aligned their bodies, so she was all too aware of how powerfully aroused he was. Another kiss sent her world spinning out of control until she was limp and clinging to him. That was when he stunned her by ending the kiss with the same startling abruptness with which he'd begun it.

Breathing in savage bursts, his hands fell to his sides and clenched.

"What?" she whispered. "What's wrong?"

"That's for you to say. I don't want you to regret this tomorrow."

"Don't you want me?"

In the deep shadows his eyes glittered. "Yes, I want you," he growled. "How can you even ask?"

When he didn't touch her again, she knew he must be giving her the chance to change her mind.

But for the life of her, she was helpless against the tide of desire that swept her. From the first moment he'd returned to the ranch, some force had taken over. It possessed her utterly now. She'd always wanted him. She'd measured all other men by him, even after her mother had convinced her he was no good.

She'd wanted him more each day he'd been here. She'd been lonely for this, for him, for too many years. She was only human. How long could she fight the inevitable? If he'd gone that first day without ever finding out about Daniel, then maybe she would have been safe. But now that he knew the truth and she saw how much Daniel needed him, she couldn't regret that he'd found out.

She knew Luke didn't love her and that almost certainly he never had. But in this moment all that mattered was the sexual joy she'd know if she slept with him again, if only for one night.

She hurled herself into his arms, and he caught her against his naked chest, crushing her close. "Darling," he whispered in a low, raw tone that thrilled her. "Sweetheart. I want you so much. But I won't pressure you."

"I can't fight what I feel for you any longer."

He pushed her against the wall, kissing her until her heart raced and she could barely breathe. She knew he was wrong for her. Still, she clung to him, never wanting to let him go…because she knew too well the loneliness of being without him. Six long years she'd lived here without this man's love. "I want you more than anything," she whispered. *Despite everything.*

"Okay, then…."

Lifting her into his arms, he carried her to his bedroom. He kicked the door shut and threw the bolt. Then he swept her down onto his bed.

"Take off your clothes," he ordered in a deep, hoarse voice that caused her to shiver.

She tore off her robe. Then she lifted her nightgown and flung it away. "Beautiful," he rasped. His eyes devoured her as he ripped off his pajama bottoms.

"You're beautiful, too," she whispered as she studied his broad shoulders, rippling torso and huge erection. "So beautiful."

He lay down beside her and stroked her breasts, and tongued her navel. Her nipples hardened and goose bumps pricked all over her belly. "When I left you that note and found you in bed naked and looking so adorably sexy, it was all I could do not to kiss you awake."

Adorably sexy. With a shy smile that probably gave too much away, she turned her face fully toward his. She had hoped he'd felt something like that for her.

"Adorable," he repeated. Gathering her closer, he kissed her passionately.

At the contact with his hard lips and naked skin, she trembled. His body was warm and muscular. His obvious desire made her feel loved and safe, but, of course, that was an illusion.

Something to worry about tomorrow...

Better to focus on the burning thrill of his hands and mouth, better to abandon herself to this soul-deep need he had taught her to want, better not to worry about the consequences.

But they would come eventually.

In no time, his mouth and hands took her beyond anything she'd ever experienced or imagined, even with him. As his tongue laved her, she arched her body into his. Soon she was lost in the white heat of a passion that left her shattered. Afterward, all she could do was lie limply in his arms, her fingertips splayed across his chest feeling every beat of his heart.

Their first night together, so long ago, she'd been limited by her shyness and inexperience. Now she knew that no one else could ever make her feel like he did—rapturous, ravaged, cherished and utterly satisfied.

She loved him. Fool that she was—she always had. Not that she'd been proud of loving him, after the way they'd parted. Still, he'd been sweet to her when she'd been a girl, and ever since he'd come back, he'd taken care of her and Daniel, amazing her with the depth of his feelings for his son.

Even so, being older, she should know that gratitude and sexual attraction and having a son together were not enough for a solid relationship. She should have resisted temptation.

Easy to say, when not faced with Luke and her own needs. When he again kissed her lips as hungrily as he had out in the hall, she did not resist. The second time was even better than the first.

When it was over, she lay beside him, feeling faint and shaken. Wrapped by the darkness and their body heat, neither spoke. She could only wonder what he thought and felt. She didn't ask, since she feared the worst.

Why had he slept with her? Would he be finished with her now? Would he announce his solution and then leave? Did he now feel free to marry the perfect Teresa?

A strange desolation stole over her heart. She was such an idiot to want him, and then to sleep with him, especially when he had final say over the fate of Wild Horse Ranch. But could one control one's feelings?

She closed her eyes, willing herself to sleep and forget, but such peace did not come easily. This night in his arms had heightened his power over her. She knew she would want him again, and again. She wanted him to love her, to stay with her, to be an ordinary rancher rather than a glamorous billionaire.

But that was not possible. So somehow, when he informed her of his plans to get her ranch on sound footing, she would find the strength to let him go.

Eight

This was one of those moments in life that was so perfect she wanted to seize it and make it last forever.

Cool air seeped through the ancient wooden windowpanes, bringing with it the sound of morning doves. Soon it would be time to get up and get Daniel ready to catch his bus.

Drowsily Caitlyn lay still, savoring this fleeting moment. It was delicious to just remain under the covers, nestled close to Luke's blistering warmth. All too quickly his watch alarm went off.

He rolled over and kissed her lips. "Time to get up, sweetheart," he drawled in a lazy voice, his heated breath tickling her earlobe.

"Hmm," she murmured. For another long, delightful moment Caitlyn lay where she was, her eyes closed, not wanting to face the day or its realities. She hadn't slept so blissfully in years.

"If you don't get up, Daniel will find you here in my bed," Luke whispered. "Is that what you want?"

"Of course not." Not that she liked being reminded that her presence in his bed might be a shameful thing in other people's opinions. Her eyes snapped open and she forced herself to sit up and focus.

He seemed so cool and businesslike this morning. Leaning down, he picked up her nightgown and handed it to her.

Feeling uncertain, she pulled it over her head. Then she stood up and grabbed her robe, tying the sash.

"We'll talk later," he said.

"About your mysterious solution?"

His expression darkened. "Did you sleep with me thinking I'd go easier on you when it came to sorting out your ranch's problems?"

"No!"

His green eyes seared her.

"No!" she whispered, feeling guilty even though she didn't have a reason to. "How can you ask me that?"

"Easy."

"Maybe you're like that, but I'm not."

"Okay. I'll take your word for it. Let's leave it at that."

She hated the distance he was deliberately putting between them.

"When are you planning to go back to London?" she asked.

He frowned. "Sooner than I'd like. There's a crisis brewing in one of my more recently acquired companies."

At the thought of him leaving for good, a raw, aching loneliness swamped her. So she played dumb. "Oh, that's what that phone call last night was about?"

"Yes. Although, I would have sworn you were hovering right outside the door, hanging on to every word. I hope I didn't sound too tough."

She blushed. "Maybe I did glean that some of your new employees see you as a tyrant."

He exhaled a sharp breath. "There are necessary adjustments that must be made for that company to be viable and competitive in the global marketplace. I'll explain later."

She nodded. Without a word, she crossed the room and opened the door to leave him.

He touched her shoulder and pulled her back for a spontaneous kiss. When she jerked away, he said, "Caitlyn, I'm sorry we seem to have gotten off on the wrong foot this morning. Is something else the matter?"

"Like you said…I'd better go before Daniel wakes up and finds me with you."

"Right."

She scampered down the hall on her tiptoes, but stopped short in her own room at the sight of her reflection in her mirror. Her dark hair was wildly matted; her eyes looked bruised. Fighting tears of humiliation, she swallowed. She was sure last night hadn't meant much to Luke, and she felt ashamed that he might suspect the depth of her feelings for him.

Despite the problems with the ranch, she'd seen herself as a strong person. She'd survived Luke's betrayal, a marriage of convenience to a man who hadn't been able to love her as a real husband, her parents' deaths and then Robert's illness and death. She'd lived with pressing financial burdens as a single mother. But once Luke reappeared she'd realized just how vulnerable she'd always been…alone out here with no family other than Daniel. And needy, at least where Luke was concerned.

Last night in his arms she'd felt a rush of joy such as she hadn't felt since her parents' and Robert's deaths. But what was such foolish happiness based on if all he'd felt was lust?

Soon, he'd issue some unpleasant ultimatum concerning her ranch and darling horses. Then he would leave her to deal with her options. Luke would leave and be glad to be gone, and she would go on, alone. Still, the sooner the business between them was over, the better. Because every day and every night that she spent with him, she would only fall more deeply under his spell.

Moving slowly, she showered and dressed. Vaguely she was aware of Luke telling her through the door that he'd made coffee and would see to Daniel. Thinking how nice it was to have him do fatherly things for Daniel, her attitude toward him softened even more.

Still, because she was determined to avoid him, she tarried so long in her room that when she finally came out, the house was empty.

Somehow she had to make him tell her the solution to her business problems so she could end this—before it got any more complex.

He shouldn't have slept with her.

But how could he have stopped himself?

Maybe sex was a basic mammalian function, but it always complicated the hell out of everything.

After dropping off Daniel at the bus stop, Luke drove Caitlyn's truck up to the house and braked in a whirl of dust. Reluctant to face her for reasons he didn't analyze, he cut the ignition. Out of the corner of his eye he saw furtive movement at the kitchen window, but when he turned his head the curtains snapped together.

Clearly, she was in no mood to face him, either.

The sex had been so great last night, he'd thought their connection might help his case. But as usual, Caitlyn hadn't reacted as he'd expected. She'd been so moody and unpredictable this morning, he now wished he hadn't lost control.

He was in a bind. Because of the crisis in London, he had to get back. He'd run out of time to woo her or cajole and explain. But because of Daniel he wasn't about to go away without clarifying their situation. Daniel needed a man in his life. Her business was going under. She needed Luke's skills, his money and his support, with Daniel and in her business.

He'd decided to offer her marriage in exchange for such help.

No doubt Hassan had bankrolled her ranch primarily because he was sure Luke would help her once he knew about Daniel. So, knowing Hassan would support whatever decision he made, Luke wanted to step in and take over as soon as possible.

When the thought of marrying her had first occurred to him, he'd been stunned to realize how old-fashioned he was. Why bind himself to a woman who'd treated him so badly?

But there was Daniel, who needed a father, and Luke, who knew too well what it was to be fatherless. His childhood had been bleak after his mother had left. Maybe for that reason he'd always idealized families where both parents stayed together and raised their children.

He'd already missed five years of Daniel's life, and he didn't want to miss any more or to divide Daniel between them in a custody arrangement.

Still—marriage? In this modern time surely there was a better, easier way for him to help her and become a part of his son's life? But he had to admit that this wasn't a logical decision. From the moment he'd seen Caitlyn, a widow now and free to marry, he'd known his powerful feelings for her were far from dead.

For years, jealousy over her marriage had consumed him. That emotion and the love he'd felt had eaten at him for so long it had separated him from all other women, including Teresa. He wished he didn't feel so strongly for Caitlyn, but against all logic he wanted her by his side.

He didn't know why he felt so deeply. Maybe it was because they were linked by this land and culture. In London he always felt edgy and alienated. Here, with her, he was his true self. He'd always been ashamed of being Bubba's son, of not being good enough for Caitlyn, according to her mother.

Well, he was rich now, and proud of it. He was in a position to solve all of Caitlyn's problems.

Daniel might be the catalyst behind his proposal, but Luke wanted to share his life and wealth with Caitlyn. He knew his proposal would be ill-timed and ill-received, but the fact that he'd once loved her and that he was still so strongly attracted to her made him hope that he could forget how poorly she and her family had treated him. Perhaps she would see him as the man he'd become instead of the man her mother had thrown off the ranch.

For six years, the memory of Mrs. Cooper's gloating had taunted him.

"She's with Robert Wakefield, who can offer her way more than you ever could. If you love her as you say you do, you'll collect your pay and leave. All you'll do if you stay is ruin her life, and ours, too. Your own mother ran away. Do you want to make Caitlyn so miserable she'll do the same?"

Hurt by Mrs. Cooper's words, hurt that Caitlyn preferred Robert Wakefield, he'd left in a rage. A few weeks later, he'd decided to hear Caitlyn's side, so he'd called. Her mother had answered with the news that Caitlyn was happily married to Wakefield.

Jealousy had torn through him. Luke had slammed the phone down, believing he'd lost Caitlyn because he'd been poor. Ambition born from that pain had driven him to great heights. He vowed to become more than the nothing Mrs. Cooper believed him to be.

Well, he wasn't nothing anymore.

Now he frowned, hating wanting Caitlyn so much but clear about what he had to do. He headed up the stairs, into the house. Crossing the living room, he strode into the kitchen.

Her back was to him when he banged open the door.

When she stiffened instead of turning to greet him with a smile, his stomach clenched.

After last night he felt like wrapping her in his arms and kissing her endlessly, but her coldness stopped him.

"The bus was right on time." What an inane thing to say, he thought, but how should he begin when she was clearly in a snit?

"Was it?" she replied indifferently.

"About last night," he began, warmth stealing into his voice as erotic visions swamped him.

"Right! Last night!" She jumped back as if he'd struck her. Then she whirled around and placed both hands on her hips. "Don't worry. I know it was just sex…and that all we have is Daniel and that you have your Teresa and your real life in London."

"Hey. Wait a minute—"

"No, you wait! I know last night didn't mean anything. You said you wanted to get me out of your system."

"That's not how I feel."

"I'm a big girl! You don't owe me anything. I told you from the first all I want is for you to leave! I think last night proves we should finish our business and get back to living our own lives, before we drive each other even crazier."

His heart pounded with astounding violence. How could she dismiss him and what they'd shared last night so carelessly? He'd never felt half so much for any woman, and he'd come in here to ask her to marry him. Where was the passionate woman who'd come alive in his arms last night?

Suddenly he hated all those tender emotions and craven feelings that woman had aroused in him. His gaze narrowed. With extreme difficulty he masked his anger and fierce hurt and fought to appear as indifferent and cold as she believed him to be.

"I understand how you feel," he said. "But unfortunately we have a son."

"Yes, well, I don't find his existence as unfortunate as you do," she snapped.

"You know what I mean. I'm thrilled with Daniel. I love him. I'm only sorry I didn't know about him sooner."

She tilted her chin defiantly. "So you mean now

that you're so high and mighty, you hate feeling connected to me, just as much as I hate feeling connected to you."

Last night was beginning to feel like a dream. Was he a fool to care so much for her? To want to give her another chance?

Her face and lips were bloodless. But her eyes, which for a moment reminded him of her mother's, blazed with what he took for passionate dislike.

Hell, no, he didn't hate being connected to her, but her harsh words and look made him mask his pain with cruelty. Pride made him swallow any tender confession he might have made. She'd just become the last woman on earth he'd ever reveal his true feelings to.

After investigating her situation here, he'd admired her hard work and the gambles she'd taken to make Wild Horse Ranch succeed. She'd worked herself to the bone. Why, her palms were as rough as Manuel's. But she had pluck and more determination than most of his executives. She was a good mother to Daniel, too. Sure, she'd had a run of bad luck with some of the mares she'd bought, but she had a fighting spirit and a determination to succeed. That went a long way with him.

It didn't bother him one bit that she wasn't rich. He hadn't started off with money, either.

The past was a negative he didn't like revisiting. But she'd been young and probably easily persuaded by her mother and by her family's need to get the ranch back. Caitlyn's courage and passion for horses and her accomplishments since her parents' deaths were heroic.

Bottom line: he'd admired her—immensely— until two seconds ago. Now, raging anger momentarily consumed every positive feeling he'd had when he first walked into the kitchen.

"I may hate the connection every bit as much as you do, but I'm asking you to marry me anyway. And in case you don't realize it, since you don't like the other choices we already discussed, you have no better option. Daniel is my son. Because I owe him, I'll bail you out of your financial mess."

"What?"

"You heard me. I'm asking you to marry me."

"Well, for your information, I don't want your charity."

"Maybe I don't want to give it. Neither of us has a choice."

"Surely we could work out something else."

"I think Daniel would be better off if his parents didn't live on opposite sides of the ocean."

"What about your glamorous Teresa?"

"Collateral damage."

"Just like that you'd dismiss a woman who's perfect for you to marry a woman you dislike?"

"Just like that," he growled.

"Daniel's in school."

"Kindergarten."

"Well, I won't marry you! You're the last man on earth I'd ever willingly choose!"

"And you're the last woman I'd choose." *Liar,* he thought even as he said it. "But you will marry me. Or eventually, you'll lose Wild Horse Ranch and everything else you've worked so hard for— just like your father did."

When she whitened, he hated himself for that empty threat. The reality was he'd probably save her horses when it came to that—for Daniel's sake. But he didn't stop.

"Your precious horses simply are not worth the cost of such care. As I said, you have no better option than marriage to me. You do hold the trump card—Daniel! Think about that! You're good in bed, too, and that's a talent that means something to a man like me."

"Good in bed." She hissed in a breath.

He hated himself in that moment. He hadn't meant to propose like this, angrily, tastelessly and without any gentleness, but it was done. Maybe it was just as well. Knowing how she felt, he was damn glad he hadn't groveled.

Outside, a car door slammed. Luke and Caitlyn were too busy mulling over their anger and hurt feelings while glaring at each other to pay any attention.

Light footsteps ran up the stairs outside. A fist banged on the door. Then Lisa cried jauntily, "Caitlyn?"

"Damn," Luke growled under his breath.

The front door opened and Lisa stepped into

the living room as only a good friend who was very sure of her welcome would. "Caitlyn?"

"She's in the kitchen," Luke yelled stonily.

"Oh, hi there, handsome." Lisa was all smiles as she simpered into the kitchen, carrying a sheaf of papers under one arm. "You're just the man I was looking for."

She was dressed in a tight white sweater and an even tighter pair of jeans. Her long-lashed glance darted from his drawn face to Caitlyn's. "Hey, am I interrupting something?"

"Nothing important," Caitlyn said in a tone that further infuriated Luke. "*He's* through saying what he came here to say."

"You sure you're doing okay, girlfriend?" Lisa asked. "You don't look so hot."

"Doing great," Caitlyn replied.

"Good. I'm glad to hear that. But I really came over to see Luke." She batted her lashes up at him. "It's about these old papers my bank sent me. It's business stuff. I thought maybe Luke, being so smart and all, could help me."

"Sure," he said. "Anytime. Helping a woman in distress is my special calling."

"Did you hear that, Caitlyn? Sounds like your banker sheik pal sent the right man to help you out of your jam."

Luke beamed. Caitlyn gave them both a scorching look and turned away haughtily.

"Just a minute, Lisa," Luke said as he strode over to Caitlyn.

Putting his mouth close to Caitlyn's ear, he murmured, "You think about my proposal, sweetheart. Al Johnson and the team he's assembled can be here to take over for you in a heartbeat. They'll take good care of your horses and cattle operation until we can make some other arrangement."

"He's already assembled a team? You let him do that behind my back?"

"I want an answer by tonight to my proposal. Because tomorrow I'm returning to London with or without you. Marry me, and this place you love will be free and clear. Your horses will be fine."

"But I won't be here with them!"

"I said we'll work something out on that score! Look at it this way. If you don't marry me, you'll only go deeper into debt until you strain Hassan's patience to the breaking point. Eventually, unless someone like me gifts you with a lot of cash, which is unlikely, you'll have to sell land, or horses, or your entire operation. Every month that passes, your bargaining position weakens. Trust me—without my help, or drastic cuts, you will lose this place that you love so much. And you'll force a custody arrangement that will be difficult for Daniel. None of that has to happen. If you marry me, Daniel will have a father, and you will have Wild Horse Ranch. Your horses can move to the U.K."

"And what will you get out of the bargain?"

"Daniel. *And you.* Don't ever underestimate the value of your appeal to me, sweetheart." When he stroked her cheek with a caressing fingertip, his blood pumped much too violently for his liking. "You were my first love, remember. I want you very much."

She shook her head. "I'll never believe that!"

"Then think about last night. I wanted you, and if you didn't want me just as much, you put on a damn good act."

"Luke!" Lisa called from the door in a husky, flirtatious tone. "I'm waiting, sweetie!"

Caitlyn hissed under her breath, "You'd better go, *sweetie*. Your admirer's getting impatient."

Nine

Marriage to Luke? Why had he asked *her* to marry him when he'd hesitated about marrying Teresa, who was supposedly so perfect for him?

Because of Daniel, of course. Because he felt obligated.

His proposal had Caitlyn's emotions in such a snarl that she could do nothing but think about what he'd said.

The day got worse. Lisa stayed all morning, flirting with Luke outrageously while he helped her fill out her papers at the kitchen table. Caitlyn was furious that she felt jealous. A man who was as rich and handsome as Luke was could have any woman. It increased her irritation that, no matter what he said, the only reason she could possibly find for him to ask her to be his wife was because of Daniel. His desire for her would be no reason to propose.

The sound of his deep, kind voice as he explained the papers to Lisa so annoyed Caitlyn she slammed out of the house to work in the broodmare barn.

Not that she could concentrate on her beloved broodmares once she got there. She was so mad she almost wanted him to go and live his perfect life with his perfect girlfriend so maybe someday she could forget him. Too bad his relationship with Teresa wasn't her only problem. There was also Daniel and his need for his father. And the future of Wild Horse Ranch. She couldn't go on as before, even if she didn't marry Luke.

And she didn't want to marry Luke under these circumstances. She knew too well how easily a marriage of convenience could falter. But what better choice did she have? She didn't find the idea of selling land and livestock and figuring out a new career all that appealing, either. And what about Daniel? Would she be able to make enough to take care of him, or have the time to give him all the right opportunities? He needed a mother and a father, and she was beginning to believe Luke really wanted to fill the parental role.

Still, she wanted a loving marriage, and Luke hadn't mentioned love. Loving him made her vulnerable where he was concerned. How could she live with him as his wife and survive emotionally?

Later that afternoon Luke was on the phone with his executives in London when it was time to meet Daniel's bus, so Caitlyn went.

"Where's Luke?" Daniel demanded as he piled into her battered truck with his backpack. "I like his limo a lot better than this old truck. He's got neat stuff—water and colas and real nice seats."

"You know he gave up the limo, and besides, he's on the phone. He's got a problem with one of his businesses."

Daniel kicked his backpack onto the floorboard. In no hurry to return to the house or Luke, she opened Daniel's folder to see what his homework might be. The page that fell out was a drawing of a man and a woman and a little boy under which his teacher had written the word *family*. The man had green eyes. The woman had long black hair. In between them was a kid with green eyes the exact same shade as the man's.

Caitlyn's stomach knotted as she examined the picture, which was obviously of Luke, Daniel and herself.

"Did you do this today?" she asked.

"I was s'posed to draw a family."

"Who are these people?"

"That's Luke," he said in exasperation, jamming a finger at the stick figure with the green eyes.

"And the mother?"

"You! Mom, do you think Luke could ever be my new daddy?"

Desperately, she swallowed. Then, without thinking, she wadded the paper up and threw it on the floorboard. "No! Not in a million years!"

"But Mom!"

"Buckle your seat belt!"

"But you tore up my picture!"

"I'm sorry! I truly am. I-I'll straighten it out." She leaned down, picked it up and began smoothing it. Then she handed it to Daniel.

"You ruined it! It's all wrinkled!"

"I'm sorry," she said again. "Maybe you could draw another one," she whispered in a low, choked tone.

When he didn't say anything, she turned on the ignition and drove home much faster than usual.

"Why couldn't you marry him?"

"I don't want to talk about Luke! We were doing just fine before he showed up!"

"Well…I wouldn't mind if you did…marry him," he said with equal force. "'Cause I like him. A lot! The bus driver says we look alike. And Luke said that if he had a little boy of his own, he'd want him to be just like me."

"He said that?" Her voice sounded scratchy.

"He said he couldn't ever like any boy better than me. Not even his own kid."

Her stomach felt tight. This was all Luke's fault, she thought irrationally. He should never have come back!

Knowing that she was being unfair, she shut

her eyes. In her heart she knew Luke and Daniel belonged together. Luke would make a wonderful father. She didn't want to remember how Daniel used to follow Robert around only to be rebuffed most of the time.

Perhaps it would have been simpler if Luke had never kissed her, or made love to her. Or shown her the truth—that she was still in love with him. He belonged in his glamorous world in London with an equally glamorous wife. She couldn't be that wife—no matter how much some secret part of her longed to be at his side. Luke had risen to heights that made a true marriage between them impossible.

How would she get through this?

By living one hour at a time, one day at time, until finally the pain dulled.

She brushed away the single tear that slid down her cheek.

Oh, what a mess she'd made of everything!

"Are you two mad at each other?" Daniel asked too brightly.

At the dining room table, Caitlyn sat stiffly

across from Luke and a platter of fried chicken and mashed potatoes.

Silence.

"Of course not," Caitlyn finally managed, since Luke refused to answer.

"Then why won't you talk to each other? And why'd she tear up the picture I drew of you?"

Luke's hard gaze slid across the table to her. "Maybe because I've asked your mother to marry me," he said quietly.

"What?" she gasped, glaring at him.

"This is great! Are you going to, Mom? Are you going to?" Daniel cried eagerly.

"I can't believe you would do a thing like that! You have no right to involve him," Caitlyn cried.

"Why not?"

"Why not? How can you ask me that? He's a small child, that's why! It's unfair to involve him!"

"It's a family matter, and he's a very important part of the family."

"But Mom, I already told you I want him to be my new daddy."

"There," Luke said, "it's settled. The vote is two against one."

"It is not settled," Caitlyn said. "Not by a long shot. This is not a democracy. I decide who I'll marry. Or, in this case, who I won't marry."

Luke grabbed her hand and reached for Daniel's. "So, will you marry me?"

Twin pairs of green eyes burned her.

"Do it, Mom! Please!" Daniel whispered.

It seemed unfair, the two of them working together this way.

"All right." She finally relented, unable to say no to the pleading in Daniel's gaze. "I'll marry you."

Daniel threw himself in her arms, and she hugged him tightly. Not that she dared so much as glance at Luke.

So, it was settled. Because she'd made such a tangle of her life; because Luke wanted to be a full-time father and would be good at it; because Daniel, who'd always craved a father, wanted Luke to be his father so much.

And because she loved Luke and couldn't bear

to see him go away to London, knowing she would never see him again.

Maybe he didn't love her. Maybe she couldn't measure up to the perfect Teresa or be the wife a man like him needed, but if she didn't try, she'd never forgive herself.

No sooner had he gotten Daniel into bed than Luke knocked on Caitlyn's bedroom door.

She cracked the door half an inch. Her eyes were wet looking. Had she been crying? Because of him?

"You can change your mind," he said when she refused to meet his eyes.

"No. I mean…yes," she whispered in a tone that betrayed her utter misery.

"Yes?"

"Yes! I'll marry you! Like I told both of you earlier!"

"You remember what I said about you being good in bed? You know this will not be a marriage in name only?"

"Yes, I understand what marriage means."

"Then you'll share my bed? Willingly?"

His heart sped up. After a long moment she nodded. "If you insist."

"I insist. So—prove it."

"Now?" She let out a breath.

"Kiss me. Show me that you belong to me," he said.

"But we're not married."

"After last night, does that matter?"

She closed her eyes, curled her fingers tightly.

Did she dread his touch? Maybe, but when he pushed the door wider and reached for her, she did not resist him.

"Touch me," he whispered, trying to hide his eagerness. He stepped further into her bedroom and shut the door. "Touch me everywhere."

When her chin notched up an inch, he thought she would defy him. But she didn't.

As her rough hands roamed gently over his body, his anger began to subside. In its place came that loathsome tenderness he'd felt last night, showing him how deeply he desired her good opinion. This was the girl who'd followed him around in his youth, the girl who'd given him her virginity, the girl he'd adored. When she was his wife, he would take care of her. If their marriage worked out, she would have to move her horse operation to the U.K. and visit Wild Horse Ranch only a few times a year, but he did not intend to let her work so brutally that she ruined her hands. He would buy her pretty things.

But right now, he refused to think about the future or the power she held over him. Instead, he drew her to the bed and laid her beneath him. He would think about her warm hands undressing him, stroking and caressing and circling him. Then, much to his surprise and delight, she placed her wet mouth where her hands had been and sucked deeply.

He groaned in ecstasy. Placing his hands in her hair, he spoke words he'd never intended to say, but because he felt so much for her, he could not stop himself.

When he was close to the edge, he pulled her beneath him and plunged deeply inside her, claiming her as his own.

When her arms tightened around him and she clung to him mindlessly, pleasure such as he had never known filled him. He swelled even bigger against her velvet warmth until he thought he'd die.

He didn't want her to feel this good; he didn't want to desire her this much. But treacherous feelings mushroomed inside him. She was slick and hot and tight. With every stroke, his tumultuous, conflicted feelings grew until they all but overwhelmed him. Maybe he and Caitlyn could find a way to make their marriage work.

"Caitlyn."

Tilting her head back, she stared into his eyes. Whatever she saw in their depths made her heart stampede. With a sigh, she fused her mouth to his and kissed him deeply. As he exploded inside her, he whispered her name over and over again.

At least in the bedroom, if nowhere else, she was his.

Caitlyn stared moodily out the window at the glittering Las Vegas strip. Vegas was the last place she'd ever thought she'd marry.

After making love to her last night Luke had held her close and said they should get married in Vegas before going to London.

"Why Vegas?" she'd whispered uneasily.

"Because it's fast and easy. Because we can obtain a license and marry the same day with very few questions asked. We have enough problems, don't you think? The first one being you and Daniel moving away from your home on very short notice."

"And leaving my horses."

"Temporarily. We'll figure out something. All the more reason why we don't need the stress of planning a wedding."

"But none of our friends or family will be there to celebrate with us."

He'd shot her a quick, dark look, and she'd remembered he didn't consider their marriage a celebration. For him, it was an obligation.

"Okay, since you hate the idea of such a wedding, I'll make all the arrangements," he'd said. "We'll have to delay our trip to London by a day or so."

"But how can I leave the ranch? It doesn't run itself, you know. I have to pack."

"I hired Al Johnson and his team. They'll be here first thing in the morning."

"You were that sure I'd say yes."

"Yes was your best option."

So here she was in Vegas, alone in one of the fanciest hotels on the strip, waiting for Luke and Daniel to return from buying a wedding license. Making use of her time, she'd dressed in a stunning off-the-shoulder black dress that Luke had bought for her. As gorgeous and practical as the dress was, she couldn't help remembering the white gown she'd worn when she'd married Robert. Because of her mother, her first wedding had been completely traditional.

Eyeing the bottle of champagne Luke had placed on ice for later, she paced restlessly.

Where was he? Was he losing his nerve?

Finally, when another half hour passed and he still didn't arrive, she went over to the chilled bottle and popped the cork.

Why wait when she needed to fortify herself for a ceremony that would probably be in some tawdry Vegas chapel?

Pouring herself a glass, she lifted it and made a silent toast to love and luck. Then she sipped slowly. Maybe, by some miracle, things would work out and they'd be happy. She imagined Luke coming home and sharing his day, preparing an evening meal together, making love. They'd do things with Daniel, have friends over like a normal couple. Maybe they'd go to parties, and to children's birthday parties, and take family vacations. She hoped so.

Somehow it was easier to imagine him working all hours while she struggled with loneliness and homesickness. Luke would prefer his glittering crowd to a simple evening with her and Daniel.

As the bubbly liquid slid down her throat, she stalked the lavish penthouse suite, stopping to stare out the tall windows, where the sight of the gaudy city slammed her again. This city with its glittering lights and glittering women was all about easy money and easy virtue, not true love. What chance did their marriage have?

Suddenly Caitlyn heard a key and then the door opened. Luke was back with Daniel, who bounded inside shouting her name. No sooner had her little boy hugged her than he pushed free of her clinging arms, anxious to show her a new toy Luke had bought him at the children's museum.

"Look. It's a propeller on a stick. If you twirl the stick in your hands, it flies. See!"

Indeed it did, skittering into a chandelier and then plummeting. For the next five minutes, the three of them chased the thing about, finding it under a red velvet couch, behind a gold curtain and on the pink marble counter of the bar. Then Luke, who was elegantly clad in a dark suit, clapped his hands and put a stop to the mayhem.

"Enough. I've got the limo waiting. It's time to get this show on the road. We leave for London very early tomorrow morning."

Daniel, who was wearing a new suit Luke had bought for him, puffed out his chest importantly and grinned from ear to ear. "Luke says I can be his best man! And ring bearer! He says I'm everything!"

Over their son's black head, Luke's gaze locked with hers. She willed him to smile or say even one kind word that would give her a ray of hope.

He said, "You wanted family to play an important role at our wedding."

She smiled wistfully, liking that he'd listened, that he'd remembered. "Come here, best man, so your mother can tuck your shirttail back in your pants."

Luke laughed.

Their wedding was small. Two chapel employees served as the only witnesses in a gold-tinted sanctuary adorned with too many angels and artificial flowers. The reverend said his words in a mechanical rush.

Despite the champagne, Caitlyn felt tense and shaky. Beside her, Luke seemed aloof and cold. Daniel, however, appeared to be bursting with joy and pride. He clutched the wedding band, twisting it round and round his finger as he bounced from one foot to the other.

When the moment for the ring came, Daniel became so excited he dropped it and had to crawl under two pews to get it. When he emerged, his shirttails hung loose and his hair was rumpled. Luke knelt down to take the ring from Daniel.

"Do you want to help me slide it on your mom's finger?" he asked.

Beaming with pride and pleasure, Daniel nodded. Then their two hands, Luke's so much darker and larger, slid the gleaming band of diamonds on to her slim finger. Before she had time to get used to the first ring, Luke slid on an immense solitaire engagement ring.

"You didn't have to," she began. "It's too much."

The man officiating said in a deep, glum tone, "You may kiss the bride."

Still holding Daniel's hand, Luke turned to her and lifted her chin with a fingertip. His nearness made her catch her breath. Pulling her against his long body, his lips brushed hers briefly, yet so tenderly her heart sped up. Strange, how even the lightest of kisses was charged with heat. For one sparkling second, she thought that maybe someday all her dreams would come true.

After that gently searing kiss, Luke squeezed his thumb against her palm and smiled down at her, a warm smile that told her he remembered all their other kisses. Then he let her go and leaned down, his attention on Daniel.

"You can open your eyes now," he said to their

son, who'd been hiding his eyes while they'd kissed.

"Is it over? Are we married now?" Daniel asked.

"Yes," Luke said, his eyes burning her. "Yes. We're married."

Ten

Marriage to a billionaire.

From the moment their jet set down at Heathrow, Caitlyn's life changed so suddenly and irrevocably, she felt thrown off balance. At their hangar, two stretch limos awaited them, one to take her and Daniel to their flat and the other to take Luke to his office.

Even though she talked to Al Johnson or one of his men on a daily basis, she missed the ranch and her horses unbearably. Technically the ranch was still hers, and Luke had promised they could move the horses to the U.K. when their lives settled down in London. Still, she felt like she'd lost a big part of herself.

Their first week together passed in a breathless blur. She was dazed from jet lag, and Luke was swamped by the ongoing crisis at Kommstarr and the resulting media frenzy. At least that was his excuse for spending so little time with her and Daniel.

The phone rang all the time. Luke was constantly defending himself in interviews and convening with his PR people. She saw his face splashed across the scandal sheets and television more than she saw it at home. Somehow he found the time to hire a tutor for Daniel so that their son could keep up with his studies until he was enrolled in a new school.

During that stressful time when they were both getting their bearings, Hassan arrived in London to welcome her. He called, issuing an invitation for dinner at his suite in two nights' time.

"I have nothing to wear," Caitlyn said to Luke the morning before they were to meet Hassan. She'd learned at their first party how inadequate her wardrobe was for her glamorous new life. The paparazzi had taken several unflattering photos and made the most of their coup. One headline read The Billionaire Marries Cinderella.

"I'll have my secretary recommend a personal shopper," Luke said.

"I don't like feeling so helpless."

"You'll soon learn all that is required. If I did it, you can. Give yourself time. Meanwhile, don't forget to enjoy London with Daniel while you do. I want you both to be happy. As soon as we select a school and get him registered, he'll be in classes all day." Having said that, he'd dressed quickly and left for work even earlier than usual.

Her new personal shopper, a Mrs. Grayson, called her an hour later to set up an appointment for that afternoon. When Caitlyn hung up, the rest of the day loomed before her, empty and devoid of any responsibilities. She'd always worked. So much freedom wasn't easy. With a butler, a housekeeper, a tutor and maids, with only the long-distance management of her ranch and horse operation to occupy her once Daniel was in school, how would she make herself useful?

Maybe Caitlyn would have found London more

enjoyable if she'd been a normal bride on her honeymoon. Or even if she'd been a normal tourist who knew that after her vacation she'd be returning to Texas.

She tried to make the best of it. She took Daniel on long, lovely walks through the city.

They saw world-class museums; the city's public parks filled with nannies, children, skaters, walkers, bikers and all sorts of people sitting on benches reading or eating their lunches. But what she liked best was riding with Daniel in Hyde Park.

Daniel, however, proved to have a small boy's taste for the macabre, preferring the torture chambers of the ghoulish London Dungeon. Its squealing caged rats and dripping water beneath the rumbling trains thrilled him. He was almost equally mesmerized by the Egyptian mummies in the British Museum.

Such delights aside, the more familiar she became with Luke's lavish, over-the-top lifestyle, the more difficult it was for her to pretend she could ever fit into it. His A-list friends included celebrities, lords and their ladies, his superwealthy business associates and their bejeweled wives.

Luke had even instructed her to leave the flat by a back exit and to wear sunglasses and a wide-brimmed hat to help elude the paparazzi.

Initially, she'd protested. She didn't want to hide or to have Luke's security team accompanying her throughout the city. But Luke had made her understand that his wealth made them targets.

"If the paparazzi discover you, it's best to say nothing," he warned. "Not always easy. But just remember they try to use your words to hang you."

And then there were Luke's offices, vast and sophisticated. He didn't drive much, but his cars were numerous and luxurious. He preferred being whisked about by his chauffeurs or helicopter pilots so he could work and return phone calls. At night she and Luke were expected to attend glamorous fundraisers and business functions. But even when they were home, his penthouse flat on the Thames with its minimalist décor and view of Chelsea Harbour was not the kind of home where she and Daniel could kick back and relax. The flat brimmed with museum-quality art, and she had to watch Daniel every second for fear his curiosity would get the best of him.

She longed for trees and birds. For the vast stillness and silence of the ranch. For unobstructed views and opulent sunsets. For privacy, a commodity she'd never realized she cherished.

She thought constantly of her big darlings back home, but all too often, her daily phone calls to Al and her vet only increased her anxiety. Yesterday, the driver who'd come to pick up three two-year-olds being shipped to California had demanded that accession numbers be written on the health certificates. She'd tried to help Al locate the certificates in her disorderly files to no avail.

Then he'd put her in a real panic when he'd told her that Angel, who'd been vaccinated against strep equi, had an abscess and was being quarantined and tested for the dreaded strangles bacteria.

Terrified, she'd called her vet.

"Don't you worry," Dr. Morrow had assured

her. "We're just taking precautions. I'm ninety-nine percent sure she doesn't have it."

If only she weren't so far away, she'd thought. "Only ninety-nine percent? Not worry? The horse business has not been a gentle teacher."

"It never is, my dear. But you enjoy your honeymoon and your handsome husband."

If only she were a normal bride and life with her handsome husband was that simple.

Much to her surprise, Hassan was not alone when they were ushered into his immense suite at The Savoy. Its green marble floors, walnut wainscoting and twelve-foot ceilings were complemented by plush white couches lit softly by lamps with pale, rosy shades. Hassan sat on one of the couches with a stunning couple. The man, who was tall and dark, had eyes only for his wife. She, a slim brunette in a floating white muslin dress, wore a white gardenia in her hair. They sat so near each other, they looked like teenage lovers.

When Hassan stood up, his dark face alight

with pleasure, he embraced Caitlyn and told her she looked beautiful in her sparkling red dress.

"It is so good that you are now my honorary daughter."

She nodded as he knelt to engulf Daniel's hand in his much larger ones.

Hassan arose after a lengthy private conversation with Daniel about something the child was holding. "I must congratulate you, my son," he said to Luke. "Your wife is even more beautiful than I remembered, and Daniel is everything a man could wish for in a son. I should know."

"I owe you," Luke said. "For giving me my son."

"I never thought that in this life I could repay my debt to you."

"But you did."

"When I saw him at Keeneland I knew," Hassan said.

As the men shook hands, Daniel set a pair of plastic dragons on his plate and beamed at everybody. Caitlyn, who had specifically told him to leave the dragons in the limousine, ignored this infraction.

"Do you like London, my little friend?" Hassan asked Daniel.

"My favorite is the dungeon! It's really creepy!"

Hassan laughed. "And that's a recommendation?"

"He's five, so yes." Caitlyn smiled.

"And you? How do you like London, Caitlyn?"

"Who could not enjoy such a city? But it is very different from the life I'm used to."

"In a good way, I'm sure."

"Yes, but I miss the ranch."

"Of course you do, but you will have a long, happy life in which you will visit the ranch often." Hassan turned to Luke. "I am pleased with your solution," he said. "Very pleased. I'm just sorry you have to be distracted by business problems when you should be enjoying your beautiful bride."

"I am enjoying her," Luke said, drawing her into his arms. "Having her and Daniel here puts business into perspective."

"But I forget my manners," Hassan said, indicating the attractive couple on the sofa. Quickly, Hassan introduced everybody.

"Principe Nico Romano and his lovely Principessa Regina Carina," Hassan said. "Nico stopped by my office today and I told him about Raffi's marriage. He's an old friend of Raffi's, you see. He couldn't wait to be introduced to you."

"I met Nico when I first went to work for Hassan," Luke said. "We hit it off immediately."

"By the way, Hassan, you can cut the titles," Nico said.

"Especially mine," Regina said. "After all, I was born in America."

"But I thought all you Americans loved titles," Hassan said.

"Not so much," Regina said. "I found them quite intimidating when I first came here. In fact, I still do. I prefer not to use mine—although it does come in handy if I run into a problem making a reservation for lunch."

"Where are you from?" Caitlyn asked.

"Austin, Texas."

"I'm from Texas, too."

Regina smiled at her, radiating friendliness, warmth and acceptance.

"I'm afraid I led a very ordinary life…until I decided to vacation in Italy and fell in love with Nico. I didn't know he was a prince at first," Regina said.

"How romantic."

"Yes, it was, but in the beginning there were problems. He was a prince. I wasn't rich. Certain people in his family didn't think I was…suitable."

"That would be my mother," Nico supplied, chuckling. "She can be formidable."

"In her defense, our worlds were so different, even Nico and I thought marriage was impossible."

"What was impossible was living without each other," Nico said in a deep, husky tone, drawing Regina even closer.

"We live in London because, frankly, I like living where people speak English," Regina said.

"And it is better for us if we don't live too close to my mother," Nico explained. "She's very old-fashioned."

"I'm an immigration lawyer," Regina said.

"You work? That doesn't sound like the life of a princess."

"My mother-in-law would love you for agreeing with her, wouldn't she, darling? We have a child, a little girl. Gloriana. She's three and our precious little whirlwind. But I have to do something besides chase her around drafty palaces and attend royal functions."

"I understand," Caitlyn said.

"Nico didn't at first. I'm afraid it was up to me to bring the Romanos into the modern world."

Nico smiled indulgently, not in the least perturbed by his wife's comments.

"Where is Gloriana?" Caitlyn asked.

"She has an early bedtime, so she's home with her nanny," Nico replied.

Strangely, despite the elegance of Hassan's white-and-gold suite, the extravagance of the numerous tasseled sofas, plump chairs and hassocks, the richness of the many courses of food and wines, Caitlyn found herself relaxing long before the men were offered port. She liked these people and felt comfortable with them—even if Hassan was the richest sheik in the world and the Romanos were royalty. She especially liked

Regina, who'd transformed herself from an ordinary Texas girl into an Italian princess.

Maybe there was hope for Caitlyn, too.

"You are remarkably beautiful," Luke said when at last they were alone in their bedroom with all of London twinkling below them. At his husky voice and hot glance, her tummy flipped.

It took immense self-discipline to keep her gaze glued to a workboat making its way up the Thames. "Thanks to the help of your personal shopper, the eminently talented Mrs. Grayson," she said modestly.

His gaze slid over her in such a lingering way she blushed in anticipation of the carnal delights he was teaching her to crave.

"I wouldn't give her undue credit. Although the red and the stylish cut certainly become you, you would be just as breathtaking without them. I was proud of you tonight."

"Thank you."

"You seemed happy. All evening I found myself regretting that I haven't been able to pay you enough attention since I got home. You know how it is when you leave—everything piles up so that you're swamped doubly when you return. I will figure out how to change that."

Ripping his tie through his collar, he crossed the room and took her in his arms. All week, she'd lived for moments when they were alone. Closing her eyes so she could savor his clean, male smell, she parted her lips as he gathered her close.

"But beautiful as you are in red silk, I prefer you naked," he whispered against her ear. When he lowered his mouth to her lips, heat washed through her.

Deftly, his hand found the zipper at the back of her dress. Within an instant the fiery silk had pooled at her feet and he was carrying her to his bed. When his tongue entered her lips, her hands around his neck tightened.

"Oh, Luke…" Arching her slim body against his heavy erection, she sighed. "I need you so much."

Suddenly, she was in a bigger hurry than he was. Finding his waistband, she undid his belt. He groaned when she unbuttoned his slacks and then slid her hand inside to explore his bare skin. When she squeezed him and moaned, he inhaled a sharp breath.

"We should slow it down, make it last." Kneeling, he positioned himself above her but didn't lower his body to hers. "You are exquisite."

"No!" she whispered, arching upward, frantic to join her body to his in the most primal way.

"If you insist," he murmured.

When he finally slid inside her, she circled his waist with her hands, tugging him closer. "Yes! Yes!"

Within seconds they were moving together, up and down, faster and faster, his hard flesh plunging inside her.

The priceless paintings in the room blurred. She couldn't breathe fast enough. Her fingertips climbed his spine and dug into his neck. She wanted him desperately. All too soon she was clinging, exploding, screaming. Only after her pleasure did he find his own, and when he did, she climaxed again. For a long, shuddering moment he held her perspiring body against his own, his blunt fingertips caressing her gently.

She felt so shattered, she wept. He smoothed her hair and kissed her forehead. "Don't cry, sweetheart."

"It scares me the way the sex keeps getting better and better."

"I rather like it," he murmured. "We can do it again if you like."

"I don't like needing you so much."

"Why not? We're married, aren't we?"

Yes, but only because he'd felt obligated, she thought, wishing with all her heart that he could truly love her.

Eleven

The next morning, Caitlyn awoke blushing. Her deliciously sensual dream had involved Luke making love to her while they rode Sahara across a moonlit desert. Sighing with fresh longing for Luke, she reached across the bed to touch him, but found only his empty pillow.

Sitting up, she opened her eyes. The bedroom was bathed with soft, gray sunlight. On her bedside table lay a crisp note.

I'll make it a point to get home early, sweetheart.

So, he'd left, and she wouldn't see him for hours. Remembering his kisses and caresses, she shivered with yearning. Stretching, she ran her fingers through her silken hair. Then she grabbed his pillow and inhaled his clean, masculine scent.

She felt happy. Truly happy, for the first time since he'd come back into her life.

If he didn't love her, he was never unkind… unless, she amended, she provoked him. The thought made her smile.

Maybe he cared a little. Maybe even more than a little. He'd said he was proud of her. He'd acted as if he adored her. There was no denying that the sex last night had been extraordinary.

But they never mentioned the past. He hadn't explained why he'd taken the money and run, why he'd walked out on her without saying goodbye or why he felt justified in being angry about the past. How could she trust him and build on that trust if they couldn't talk to each other about the things that mattered?

Despite her nagging doubts, she got up, humming to herself. Checking her cell, she saw a text from Dr. Morrow with the good news that Angel had tested negative.

Wonderful, she thought. Still humming, she

showered and went to find Daniel so they could breakfast together.

She was still aglow an hour later when she and Daniel were riding in Hyde Park on the famous sand-covered bridleway, Rotten Row.

"Mom, is that great big bird a seagull?" Daniel cried as he pointed to a huge bird near a fountain. "I thought everything was s'posed to be bigger in Texas."

"Texans do brag, but no, I don't think that's a seagull…although it is some kind of seabird. Very good observation. Later, we'll have to get a bird book and look—"

Before she could complete her answer, a man yelled her name. When she twisted in her saddle, a dozen flashes went off in their faces. She gave a cry of despair when she saw the horde of reporters stampeding toward them from behind a tall hedge.

The paparazzi.

It was all the stable groom could do to hold on to Daniel's frantic horse. When Caitlyn's gelding reared, pawing the air wildly, she dealt with him in a firm, gentle manner that soon had him under control. Then Luke's security team surrounded them.

"We've got to get you both out of here," Thierry, the head of security said.

A man in ripped jeans with keen gray eyes and a long-lensed camera pushed closer and fired questions at her as he took dozens of pictures.

"Why did your husband buy Mullsley Abbey, the home he and Teresa Wellsley toured together, and then marry you?"

"No comment," Thierry said.

"Excuse me." Caitlyn blinked in confusion. "Mullsley Abbey? I don't know anything about that."

"Rumors said he intended it for Teresa as a wedding gift," the rude reporter said.

"I don't know anything about this!" she exclaimed.

"Why did he marry you?" another man in thick glasses demanded.

"What do you mean?"

"Mrs. Kilgore, did you marry him for his money?"

"No!" she said defensively. "It was his idea to

marry me! Yes, I owed money. But he's the one who offered to help *me*."

"Isn't that another way of saying you married him for his money?"

"Is the kid Kilgore's?" another asked.

"None of your business!"

Their questions and condescension were making her too furious to think. Fortunately, Thierry got between her and Daniel and the clamoring herd.

"Is he Kilgore's?"

"No comment," Thierry growled.

Quickly, he helped her and Daniel dismount. Other members of the security team attended to their mounts while she and Daniel were hustled across the lawn to the safety of a black SUV. They sped away, only to be chased by a swarm of motorcycles. Big-eyed, Daniel pressed his face to the window.

Minutes later, after having been notified by Thierry of the ruckus, Luke called her on her cell. "Are you and Daniel okay?"

"Yes," she whispered, staring at the motorcycles. "They…they said you bought a house you'd intended to give Teresa. Is that true?"

He was silent for a long moment. "No."

"But were there rumors about it being intended as your wedding gift to her?"

"Look, I'll explain everything tonight when I get home."

"But…"

"You said you're both okay. That's all that matters. We can't worry about what the press dreams up to say about us every day for the rest of our lives. They always distort everything." He said a tense goodbye and hung up.

The story broke on television early in the afternoon, before Luke got home. Every talking head in Great Britain wanted to know who billionaire Luke Kilgore really loved—the English heiress or the Texan fortune hunter with the little boy.

"I'm not a fortune hunter," Caitlyn said to the television. "I'm not!"

There were clips of Teresa on Luke's arm, which must have been taken before he'd come to Texas. She was a young, ethereal blonde, who smiled at him as if she adored him. There were clips of their visit to Mullsley Abbey and its immense deer park. After these, a clip from today of Teresa in a white miniskirt, her cheeks tear-streaked as she dashed from Luke's office building, was aired repeatedly. She was equally beautiful in tears.

Why had Teresa gone to see Luke? Had she deliberately let the bloodhounds catch her there?

The worst clip of all, if she didn't count the ones of Daniel's pale face plastered against the SUV's window, was of an angry-looking Caitlyn defending herself by saying, "It was his idea to marry me! Yes, I owed money. But he's the one who offered to help *me*."

After seeing that clip for what had to be the tenth time, Caitlyn flipped the channel in disgust only to find another story about Luke.

"Billionaire Kilgore has been in the news because too many of his employees at Kommstarr see him as a rich CEO who wants to break up their company while firing talented people," a female newscaster brayed in an accusatory tone. "Here's what one single mother who lost her job this week has to say about him." She handed the microphone to a pretty young woman in tattered jeans, who was bouncing a crying blue-eyed baby in her arms.

"That's right. I'm a single mum, I am. Where will the likes of me go in this job market? Kilgore is filthy rich, but he's got no heart. I pity those two women, the countess and the gold digger, who are fighting over him. He may be Mr. Moneybags, but he'll break their hearts, same as he broke mine. And my little girl's. Just look at her—poor lamb. How am I going to feed her?"

Behind Caitlyn, the front door slammed. She whirled just as a haggard Luke stepped into the room. His shoulders sagged as he leaned his briefcase against the wall.

"Nothing those people are saying is true. Not a word," he said quietly. She noted the dark circles under his eyes.

"Of course," she whispered. "I believe you."

The next clip was again that of the furious Caitlyn.

A muscle jerked in Luke's hard cheek.

"That's out of context," she whispered defensively.

"I'm sure it was. I told you they'd twist anything you said or did. Why did you talk to them?"

"Because they asked me questions."

He crossed the room, grabbed the remote and turned off the television.

"What about Mullsley Abbey? Is it true? Were you intending it for Teresa before you found out about Daniel?" she asked.

"No. I visited it with her once as a regular tourist, and then I found it was for sale and became interested in it. Caitlyn, I married you. Not Teresa. I want to forget the past. I want us to start over."

"For Daniel's sake?"

"Not just for his sake, but for ours, too."

"Did you buy Mullsley Abbey?"

"Yes. For us."

She swallowed. Not that the hard lump in her throat dissolved.

"And what about Teresa? Did she come to see you today?"

"Yes."

"Did you know she was coming?"

He nodded. "She called me yesterday."

Yesterday? So, last night when he'd held her

in his arms and made love to her, he'd known he would see Teresa today. Had he been trying to manipulate Caitlyn with sex?

"Did you tell her that you felt like you had to marry me…because of Daniel?"

"No, because that's not the only reason I married you. Look, I'm sorry that I'm getting so much negative publicity right now. The takeover makes me a hot news item, so that makes you… us…and Teresa…into a secondary story—an imaginary love triangle."

Imaginary?

"I'm sorry about it, but I can't help it," he continued. "Are they discussing the factory I'm opening in Bedfordshire and all the new jobs there? No. The networks are after ratings—period. If I were you, I wouldn't watch the so-called news for a while."

"How else can I know what they're saying? Or what you're doing?"

"It doesn't matter," he said.

"It matters to me."

"It isn't real."

"When I see myself being quoted and accused of being a gold digger, it feels real," she said.

"You said they distorted what you meant. Well, they twist my actions, too. You know you're not a gold digger."

"Do I? You said you'd finance Wild Horse Ranch if I married you, and you did."

"I wanted you to marry me. I would have said anything or done anything to achieve that."

"But the fact is, your wealth, your ability to save the ranch was a factor in my decision to marry you. So, in a sense, I am a gold digger."

"Okay. My money's an issue, then. But that doesn't make you a gold digger. You can concentrate on the negative or the positive." He paused. "I would like to make our marriage work."

Was he telling the truth? she wondered.

"Those people are after one thing—salacious stories. They lie. They exaggerate. My fame and wealth will always make us vulnerable to this kind of attack. But fame is an illusion. It's just an opinion held by some people, all of them strangers, because I'm wealthy and own public companies. They don't know me, the man. Or you.

Or what I feel about you. What they say doesn't need to have anything to do with us."

He'd bought the house he and Teresa had looked at together. He'd known she was dropping by the office. Those facts were real.

"I don't know what to believe anymore," she said slowly.

"I've been at this awhile. My advice is don't watch this stuff. What we need is time to ourselves to adjust to our new life together."

"But we don't have that luxury," she whispered. "We live in a fishbowl with the whole world judging us. What will that kind of life do to Daniel? What will he think of you and me?"

"You're right. I should have addressed the issue sooner. We need to take steps to protect him immediately."

"What do you mean?"

"We have to tell him the truth…about who I am."

"What?"

"We've got to tell him I'm his real father. Tonight. Now."

"No! I told you. He's all mixed up about Robert. He's not ready."

"Would you prefer that he hear lies and half-truths from the kids at school? Do you want him to feel all mixed up like you're feeling? No, you were right the first time. Telling him the truth is the only way we can protect him."

Twelve

"That was one bite! Do I have to eat more?" Daniel glared at the spinach soufflé that was still on his plate as he set his fork down.

"No," said both his parents in low, icy voices.

Their cool glances met for a mere half second. Quickly, Caitlyn looked away, her eyes seeking the safety of Daniel.

"Can I leave, then?" he asked her. "Please. I want to play with my castle and dragons."

"Before dessert?" Caitlyn replied. "It's chocolate mousse."

"Okay. I'll stay."

Daniel stared at each of them and then at the

crystal chandelier above the gleaming dining room table. Luke and Caitlyn continued to eat their soufflés, which had become tasteless in the suffocating silence.

"Why do we have such a big table?" Daniel asked.

Why couldn't he just sit quietly for once? Caitlyn thought, and then realized it was hardly Daniel's fault that she felt so tense and out of sorts.

"For dinner parties," Luke replied.

"But it's always just us," Daniel answered.

"We'll have parties in the future," Luke said.

"Who'll come?"

"Our friends."

"Do you have any kid friends who could bring more toys?"

"Some of my business associates have children."

"What are their names?"

"Daniel!" Caitlyn snapped.

"What?" Daniel asked. "What's wrong with asking questions?"

"Nothing," she whispered, chastened. "Mommy doesn't feel well, that's all."

Daniel sighed. Lapsing into a silence that was almost as glum as hers, he stared up at the ceiling again. For the next few minutes there were only the sounds of glasses being lifted and set down, of silverware clinking against china. Her nerves strained to the max, Caitlyn set down her fork.

"You're doing it again!" Daniel said.

"What?" Both adults eyed him guiltily as he glanced from one to the other.

"Not talking to each other. Not looking at each other. Y'all will only talk to me. How come? Are you mad at each other again?"

"No, we have a secret we're going to tell you after dinner, and it's making us nervous," Luke said.

Caitlyn looked up at him, aghast.

"I don't know about your mother," Luke said, reaching across the table and wrapping her clenched hand in his, "but it's sure making me edgy and none too talkative."

Caitlyn tried to yank her hand free, but Luke folded his hand over hers and held on tight.

"A secret! I can't wait! Tell me now!"

"And skip dessert?" Caitlyn said, still struggling to free her hand.

"Mom, can't you tell me now and then we'll have dessert after the secret?"

"We can do anything we want to," Luke said, smiling at Caitlyn. Letting her go, he stood up.

Taking the boy's hand, who clung to him happily, he led Daniel onto the balcony. Caitlyn followed them, nervously wrapping a cashmere pashmina around herself when she began to shiver in the damp, chill air.

Sitting down, Luke drew Daniel into his arms.

"Did you know that the minute I met you, I knew you were special?" Luke began.

Daniel's big, white smile flashed as he curled more snugly into Luke's arms.

"And you are special, much more special than I realized." He smoothed Daniel's hair behind his ear. "You know I told you that your mother and I are old friends, that we knew each other before she married your father."

"Yes," Daniel murmured.

"Well, the truth is, we were more than friends. We fell in love. You are our son."

Daniel sat up straighter, looking from one to the other. "For real?"

"For real," Luke said. "I am your real father. But I didn't know it until I saw you that day in the road."

"Why didn't you tell him about me, Mom?"

"Don't blame your mother. I went away. She didn't know where I was. She married Mr. Wakefield, and you were told he was your father."

"But why? Why did you leave her and not tell her where you were going?"

"It's not that simple, but that's a story for another day."

"So that's why our eyes are just alike," Daniel said in a low, awed tone. "Everybody says so. And our hair's even the same color. But I'm not as tall as you."

"Yet. You're only five, so you'll probably grow."

"Really? So, I'll grow big and tall...just like you?"

"Maybe even taller. But only if you keep eating your spinach soufflé."

"Yuck."

"When I found out about you, I thought we

should become a family. Your mother agreed. So here we are."

"And that's the secret?"

"That's it."

"Now can I eat my chocolate mousse?"

"You've been very patient. I believe you've earned it."

"Will chocolate mousse make me grow tall?"

"Not nearly so tall as spinach soufflé," Luke said, chuckling as he rumpled Daniel's hair.

"That's not fair!"

When Daniel sprinted ahead of them to the kitchen, Luke looked at Caitlyn, whose chest felt unbearably tight. So many things in life weren't fair, she thought.

"Well, I thought that went rather well," he said, sounding pleased.

"I suppose." Her voice was barely audible, and she couldn't meet his eyes.

"So, why the long face?" he whispered, concern in his low tone.

"I'm cold. Let's go in."

"Right. Let's not talk about all the elephants in the room."

She frowned. Why did she feel like her life was spinning out of control? Why couldn't she stop thinking about the beautiful house Luke had visited with Teresa?

Why couldn't she believe Luke when he said he wanted to make their marriage work? Why was it easier to believe the vicious taunts of strangers?

"Surprise!"

Caitlyn, who'd been expecting another intimate dinner party on Hassan's plump sofas, gasped. Rather than something sparkly, for a party, she wore the simple off-the-shoulder black sheath that had been her wedding dress with a string of pearls.

When the huge throng of well-wishers in black ties and evening gowns advanced, she froze in the doorway until Luke gently nudged her forward.

A man at the back of the crowd tapped his champagne glass. "Congratulations are in order!"

"A toast! Hassan! A toast to your son, the bridegroom, and his bride."

When dozens of people lifted their champagne glasses, Caitlyn swayed dizzily against Luke.

Hassan rushed forward, took her hand to steady her and said something in flowing Arabic that Caitlyn could only suppose was a toast. When he finished, he drained his glass and threw it at the marble fireplace, smashing it into gleaming shards that caught the light from the lamps and shot golden rays of fire. Everybody else drank to the toast and broke their glasses, too.

More crystal flutes were brought on silver trays, and soon the glittering crowd surrounded them, clamoring to be introduced to Raffi's bride.

"So glad to meet you," each said in turn, pressing her hand until her fingers hurt. Thankfully, most of their conversation was directed toward Luke, whom they knew.

"So surprised when we heard Raffi got married."

"Wonderful of Hassan to throw this party so we could meet you, love."

"We thought he'd never—"

"So many different women. And all of them so

beautiful," one man said into her ear. "But you are the fairest of all."

"I'm sure," Caitlyn whispered, wishing with all her heart that she was.

"Still, you'll need to keep an eye on him, young lady," the man's wife warned.

Finally, after she'd been introduced to everyone—lords, ladies, film people, businessmen and their wives—Luke left her with Hassan, saying he'd bring her a plate of food. But a bony, birdlike woman with a teased puff of red hair pounced on Hassan immediately, saying she had something very important she simply had to tell him.

"Just for a bit, my dear. I won't keep him long."

"Gossip, no doubt, knowing Marie." Hassan winked.

Caitlyn said she didn't mind in the least and was stranded alone on the edge of the party. For a second or two she felt conspicuous and uneasy, but she wasn't alone for long.

Arm in arm, both of them smiling at each other and then at her, Nico and Regina strolled over. Then Luke appeared with plates of sushi.

Immediately, Caitlyn relaxed. If Regina could

transform herself into a princess and manage a difficult royal mother-in-law, there was hope for Caitlin, too.

"Where's Daniel tonight?" Regina asked.

"We have a new nanny."

Several pleasant moments of conversation about Glory's mischievous antics and the details of their meeting with the new teacher ensued. Caitlyn was laughing when the front door opened and a flash of shimmering white drew her attention to a lovely blonde.

A hush fell over the crowd. Beside her, Luke stiffened as if he'd been struck a blow.

"Oh, no," Regina whispered, touching Nico's arm. "It's Teresa. What's she doing here?"

The wild-eyed girl stared at Luke and then at Caitlyn for a moment that seemed to stretch endlessly. For that lifetime, it was as if they were the only three people in the room.

The girl was radiantly beautiful, but her lavender eyes held poignant desolation. Caitlyn felt both jealousy and sorrow as the girl took one faltering step toward Luke before losing her nerve. Perhaps she remembered that she hadn't been invited. She flushed. Then with a little cry, she turned and fled.

"Excuse me," Luke whispered before rushing to Teresa's side and ushering her back out the door, which closed behind them.

"Poor thing," a woman standing nearby said to her companion. "Everybody knows she's the one he really loves."

Pain stabbed Caitlyn like an ice pick to her heart. For a moment, she found it difficult to breathe.

"Why would you say that when he married Caitlyn?"

"Because I always thought they made a gorgeous couple. Teresa is so refined. She comes from such wonderful people. He bought the house he intended for her."

Caitlyn's confidence drained away.

"You can't believe everything you read."

"Well, what could a horse trainer from Texas and a man like our Luke possibly have in common? And her dreadful accent." The woman laughed. "Did you speak to her?"

Caitlyn lifted her head and tried to pretend she hadn't heard.

"You mustn't worry what other people think. Or about Teresa showing up uninvited to attract Luke's attention," Regina said gently. "Sometimes it's difficult for the young and beautiful to accept the ending of a relationship they've set their hearts on. She was so sure of him."

Because he'd made her feel secure in his love?

Caitlyn nodded mutely. She understood Teresa's pain too well. At nineteen she'd felt sure of his love, too. Then he'd left without saying goodbye.

In less than five minutes, the door opened again, and Luke strode back inside—alone. He was pale and tense, but he caught Caitlyn's eye and went immediately to her side.

"Sorry about that," he whispered tightly against her ear. When he touched her arm, she stepped away from him.

"It's okay," she said. But she didn't feel okay. She felt unsure.

Even though she tried to avoid his touch, he tucked her hand into his and brought it to his lips. "I think she's on the road to accepting our marriage."

Caitlyn bit her lips. What about Luke? What did he feel? Even though he stayed at her side for most of the evening and acted the part of a very devoted bridegroom, the party celebrating their marriage had been spoiled. At least for Caitlyn, who kept seeing the beautiful, broken-hearted Teresa searching a sea of faces only to find Caitlyn at Luke's side. Caitlyn kept seeing Luke running after Teresa. He'd put his hand on the girl's spine as he'd ushered her outside. The girl obviously adored him and was so exquisitely beautiful.

Later, when Luke left her to talk to Hassan, Caitlyn overheard snatches of furtively whispered conversations that tore her heart into more pieces.

"I hear he married her in Vegas. You can be sure his wedding to Teresa would have been a grand affair."

Luke said the press coverage didn't matter, but these people were his friends. It was obvious that they believed Teresa was the right bride for Luke. They knew him, didn't they?

Luke tried to talk to her on the way home, but she turned away and kept her face pressed against the glass of the limousine. When they had undressed and were in bed, he tried to pull her close, but she shook him off, saying she had a headache.

"That's the oldest excuse in the book," he teased, running the pad of his thumb down her spine and causing her to shiver.

"Please—just leave me alone," she whispered even as she began to ache for him.

The thumb followed the same tingling path back up to her neck. "Are you upset because of Teresa?"

"No," she lied.

"Do you want to talk?"

"No! I don't want to talk! I want to go to sleep. I'm tired. I'm not in the mood."

"Maybe I could persuade you to be in the mood," he said huskily. "I'm very good at that, you know."

His hand slid against her spine again, and she felt a familiar frisson of electricity.

"I said no," she whispered desperately.

She knew she was being unreasonable, but she couldn't stop herself. She wanted him to hold her and reassure her. She wanted him to make wild, passionate love to her, and yet…and yet she kept remembering Teresa, so she pushed him away.

Yes, she was jealous of the beautiful young girl who had loved and lost him. He'd once said Teresa was perfect, and those other women concurred. Such a woman would be better suited to the role of a billionaire's wife than she, who was homesick for her ranch and horses, who sometimes felt she would never fit in here.

Her mind raced in circles, repeating a constant refrain. She had Luke. Hadn't he said he wanted to make their marriage work? That meant he was trying to forget Teresa. She should be happy. But she wasn't. She wanted to possess his soul as he possessed hers.

He kissed her hair. "All right, then."

When he finally rolled over onto his side, she lay on hers. Crossing her arms over her breasts, she felt stiff and cold and proud and utterly miserable as she stared up at the ceiling.

He was soon asleep. She lay awake for hours, listening to his even breaths in the dark, loving the sound of them, loving him, knowing that she had to summon the courage to give him his life back.

Sometimes a woman, even a smart woman, could be her own worst enemy. Caitlyn hadn't slept well after she'd finally dozed off. She knew she shouldn't go looking for trouble so soon after waking. She should think her plan through. But riddled by her insecurities, she was in such an awful mood, she couldn't help herself.

She despised herself for craving him, hated the circumstances that had brought them back together. If only she could fit into his world as well as that lovely girl with the desolate lavender eyes.

Logically, Caitlyn knew that Luke was a grown man who had made his own choices. Fitting into his world would take time. Building a solid marriage required work and patience. But after last night, she wasn't feeling logical or patient.

When she stormed into the dining room, she found him sitting alone at the end of his long dining room table. He was reading his newspaper, eating eggs, mushrooms and bacon. He looked so tall and darkly handsome in black slacks, a white shirt and tie—so adorable.

Her heart lurched. She hated to interrupt him when he was enjoying a rare moment of solitude, but she couldn't stop herself.

"Luke."

He looked up. Did she only imagine that his eyes were shadowed with pain before he smiled pleasantly and tried to pretend nothing had gone wrong last night?

"Good morning," he said. "Feeling better, I hope?"

"This isn't working," she said, lashing into him with the fury of an unruly child. "You know it as well as I do, only I won't pretend any longer."

An edge of steel crept into his voice. "If you're still upset about last night—"

"I'm not. I'm talking about us. Our marriage.

Living together. I don't belong here. In London. With you. I can't do this. I belong in Texas."

His mouth thinned. "Look, I understand it hasn't been easy. First, you had all your ranch problems. Then I show up and propose. You give up the only lifestyle you've ever known. Adjusting to life over here took me months, years. All we've had is two damn weeks while I've been up to my ears in business crises and paparazzi."

"You need a wife more like Teresa. You said she was perfect for you."

"Well, she isn't. I'm very sorry about that embarrassing episode last night, but Teresa and I are finished. She understands that now. I think she had to see us together to get closure. You will never have to meet her again. Nor will I. Unless by accident. She's young. She will fall in love with someone else, marry and be very happy."

"This isn't just about Teresa. It's about me. I know you rescued me, okay? That was very noble of you."

"Hell, I married you because I wanted to."

"You didn't act like you wanted to."

248 MARRIAGE AT THE COWBOY'S COMMAND

"Damn it! I was angry that morning, if you'll remember."

"No. The fact is, you didn't love me six years ago, and you don't love me now!"

"Don't tell me what I feel—then or now."

"You betrayed my family and walked out on me!"

"The hell I did."

"Nothing's changed other than that you learned we have a son."

A muscle in his jawline throbbed. "I'm not having this conversation now—when you're obviously overwrought about last night."

"For the last time, this is not about last night! This is about us. We don't belong together anymore, if we ever did."

He crushed his newspaper and threw it down on the table.

"We have a child. We should think of him and what's good for his future instead of poking at old wounds."

"What I'm trying to tell you is that I'm going home—whether you like it or not."

"Just like that? What about the future of your

ranch and your horses? How will you straighten out your finances if I fire Al and his team?" He stood up and was about to walk toward her when his cell phone rang.

"Do what you like. You don't own me," she cried. "Somehow I'll figure out my future on my own."

He grabbed his phone and punched a button, silencing it. "What about Daniel? Do his feelings matter?"

"Of course they matter. More than anything." She heard the loud, furious, chopping whir of his helicopter circling before it landed on the roof above them. Obviously, she'd used up what little time he had.

"He can stay here with you for a while. We'll work out a permanent custody solution later," she said. She'd never been separated from Daniel, nor he from her, for any significant length of time. But she'd kept him from Luke for five years, and the boy had just learned Luke was his real father. To be fair to them, she couldn't rip him away while she sorted out her emotions and problems.

"So, you have it all figured out. Daniel's life. Mine. And we have no say."

"That's right. You all but forced me to marry you. I told you we were doomed from the beginning. If I leave, you are free to live the life you choose."

Above them she heard the whoosh of helicopter blades. He was probably late for an important meeting.

"Am I?" His eyes darkened with cynicism. "What if I say—I choose you."

"I would know you made that choice out of obligation, and that's no basis for a marriage."

"Maybe it's true I would never have returned to Texas if Hassan hadn't seen Daniel, but once I saw you, you mattered to me, too."

"Not enough. You've never wanted me enough. Not now and not in the past."

"Damn it, if you can believe that, I won't force you to stay. But don't tell me I didn't love you six years ago. It was *you* who walked out on *me*— probably because you and your family thought I was nothing and Wakefield was a means to get your precious ranch back!"

"That's not what happened, and you know it."

"The hell it isn't! Why do you think I've worked my ass off ever since?—it's because I didn't want to be a nobody who couldn't even hold on to the woman I loved. What irony…"

Grabbing his jacket off the back of the chair, he slung it over his shoulder and strode out of the room.

"But I didn't think you were nothing," she whispered behind him. "That's ridiculous."

If he heard her, he never looked back.

"I didn't walk out on you," she whispered defensively.

But you're walking out on him now.

She went to the window and watched the helicopter whir noisily before spiraling upward and disappearing into the thick gray clouds.

A single black carry-on stood beside the front door. There was only one thing left to do, and being a coward, she'd put it off until the last moment.

Walking down the hall, she heard Daniel in

his room playing with his toys long before she reached him.

Hesitating outside his door, she listened to his action figures threatening each other with doom and destruction.

"Daniel?" She slowly pushed his door open.

He looked up eagerly. "Are you going to play with me?"

"Not today."

"Can we go see the mummies?"

"I can't, but maybe your new nanny can. I'm afraid Mommy's going home to Texas for a while."

He went still, his green eyes clouding. "Are you going to take me with you?"

"Only if you want to go. You're my little boy. You're always welcome wherever I am. But you're Daddy's little boy, too, now."

"What about Daddy? Where will he be?"

"He is going to stay here. He has to work."

"Who will be with him besides me if you're not here?"

Teresa, maybe, she thought.

"All his friends and fellow workers."

"They don't come home with him at night."

"No, they don't. But you'll be here with him. He'll read to you and play with you just like he does every night. And anytime you want to come to Texas to be with me, I'll come back to get you."

"You will?"

She nodded.

"Then I want to stay with him, for a little while, but I don't want you to go. I want you to stay here with us."

"I can't, honey."

"But I want you here!"

"I know. I want to be with you, too. But I have to go home. To figure out some grown-up things."

His bottom lip curled dangerously. He put his action figure down and came toward her, dragging his feet. Slowly, he put his arms around her and held on for a long time.

When he finally let go, he said, "I don't want you to leave."

"I know, honey." Guilt swamped her. Her throat tightened. "See you soon," she whispered. "Real soon."

"When?"

"In a few weeks," she said, realizing there was no way she could leave him for much longer. "I promise we'll be together soon."

"I just want us all to be together like the picture I drew," Daniel pleaded in a very small voice.

"I know, honey."

"I thought we were going to be a real family."

If only she felt like her marriage to Luke could work, but in reality their lives and tastes were so different now, she didn't think their marriage could prove viable in the long run.

She hugged Daniel fiercely and then let him go.

Thirteen

Each day felt endless. She'd thought maybe the leaden pain in her heart would lessen in familiar surroundings, but without Daniel and Luke, the ranch felt like a prison cut off from the rest of the world by endless acres of grass and mesquite.

It was a struggle to get up in the mornings, a struggle to dress, to eat, to get through her work day, so she forced herself to follow a rigid schedule. In the evenings, when she finally came in from the barns, she would go to Daniel's room and sink onto his bed.

At night she would lie in his bed holding Daniel's stuffed bear, missing her son. And then she would tremble, dreaming of Luke, longing for his strong arms around her, his big body pressed against hers.

She had lied that night when she'd pushed him away. She had wanted him, ached for him, burned for him with a fever, but she couldn't believe he wanted her with the same ardor. He had married her for practical reasons, not romantic ones. He hadn't wanted to split Daniel between them. He'd said he desired her and that they could build on that. But could they, when she was so different from his glamorous friends? Wouldn't he be happier if she freed him to marry someone he loved?

When Lisa learned Caitlyn was home, she rushed over and found her in the barn brushing Angel.

"But how could you leave Luke when he's so rich and handsome? When he so obviously still loves you?"

Her last statement cut Caitlyn deeply. "I don't want to talk about it."

"Well, that's not much of a welcome," Lisa grumbled. "But I forgive you because your heart must be absolutely breaking. It's all over the internet. That Teresa he was so in love with is simply gorgeous."

Caitlyn sucked in a deep breath.

"What is she—a countess? What was it like to live the fairy tale?"

Hadn't Lisa noticed that Cinderella didn't end up with her prince?

Caitlyn brushed Angel's gleaming coat more furiously. "Lisa, I know you mean well, but don't come over here telling me what's on the internet. That's the last thing I need."

"Okay! But how could you leave Daniel? Why?"

"It's not forever. It's for a short visit. He's with his father. He needs to get to know Luke."

"Oh! Luke really is his father? Oh, my God! So, that's why you looked so sick when he first showed up! And *that's* why he married you so fast. I wondered why a rich guy like him would…"

"Thanks! I don't really want to talk about all this."

"I guess not—since you never said anything

before," Lisa said huffily. "Not even to me, your best friend."

"If I'd told you, you'd have told everyone!"

"I would not!"

"Okay. You would have told one person who would have told one person.... I did what I thought was best for Daniel."

"But how could you leave Luke after he came back and acted so smitten and then did right by you and Daniel without wasting any time?"

Had he seemed smitten?

"And I don't see how leaving is best for Daniel. It seems to me Luke's the one who's trying to do what's best for everybody. Not you."

"Luke doesn't love me, okay?"

"His eyes followed you, and he married you, didn't he? He must care about you a little. In fact, my guess is he cared a lot."

"I don't know. All he said was that he was trying to make the marriage work."

"Well, that's good. Honey, that's great!"

"He felt obligated."

"Hey, a rich guy like him isn't going to do anything he doesn't want to do. You've always been way too independent. Honey, don't you know that something like thirty percent of all men marry women because of kids? You can't walk out on a good man for a dumb reason like that! He was doing the right thing!"

"It wasn't dumb to me. I want him to be happy."

"Oh, my God! This just gets worse! You really love him! And I'd bet money he loves you, too! Are you an idiot? You walked out on a billionaire, who's the father of your child, a man you love? Who probably loves you? Girl, you're not going to get another chance like this! You've got to call him. Tell him you're sorry."

She felt so left out and alone. But she had to take this time for herself—for his sake as well as for hers.

"Girl, you don't look so good. Do you want me to get you a cola or something?"

"Yes, would you, please?"

Anything not to talk about Luke and their marriage.

Caitlyn sagged against the rough wall of Angel's stall. How would she live like this, alone—for the rest of her life—without him?

"I made it before when he betrayed my family and left me," she whispered fiercely to Angel, whose big brown eyes stared at her with understanding. "I can do it again. I just have to make up my mind and be disciplined."

Angel whinnied.

But she needed him on a more profound level than she'd ever needed anything—even the air she breathed.

Getting over him the second time was going to be much worse than the first. Back then she'd been so much younger and more resilient.

Fool—who are you kidding? You never got over him. You were kissing him like you were starved for him the first chance you got.

Feeling dazed after doing without Caitlyn for seven long days, Luke let himself into the flat. Daniel, who missed his mother unbearably during the day while Luke worked, was spending the night with Nico, Regina and Glory because the three of them were much better company than he was. Thus, Luke had the flat to himself.

The place felt drearier than a tomb. His footsteps sounded hollow as he walked across the wooden floor to pour himself a gin and tonic.

All week he'd thought about what Caitlyn had said—that he'd betrayed her parents and left her six years ago because he hadn't really loved her. The truth was, when she'd discovered she was pregnant, she'd sold herself to the highest bidder. Since he'd been poor, that hadn't been him. The unfairness of her accusations infuriated him.

Damn it. He hadn't left her. What the hell did she mean he'd betrayed her parents? Her mother had fired him and thrown him off the place. Maybe Caitlyn had put her up to it, which meant that *she'd* left *him*. He'd worked long and hard to achieve his success so no woman would ever make him feel as small and worthless as she had again. But it hadn't made any difference. She'd walked out on him again as if he were nothing. Maybe she was right. Maybe he should never have married her.

But as he sat down a new thought formed. Maybe he'd been wrong to avoid talking about the past. He'd thought it was no use whining about the lousy things that couldn't be changed.

He'd wanted to build a relationship starting from where they were now. He hadn't seen any point in arguing over what had happened. But maybe they hadn't been able to trust each other because they hadn't had a frank discussion. Maybe it didn't matter so much *what* had happened but simply that they both listen and try to understand. He'd been so intent on stabilizing their current situation, he'd been blind to the importance of acknowledging the pain of the past.

He was well into his second drink when Hassan called to invite him to dinner. Unable to face another night alone, he accepted, warning Hassan that he wouldn't be good company.

"You're right. You don't look so good, and you reek of gin," Hassan said as soon as Luke sat down at the restaurant table.

"Thanks."

"It wasn't a compliment."

"Thanks for your concern, then. Or whatever the hell it was."

"What are you going to do?"

"She left me because I made her miserable. I imagine that's why she had her mother run me off six years ago. She only married me because I practically forced her to, so I don't see a remedy. Do you?"

"Do you love her?"

"Unfortunately."

"Have you told her?"

"No."

"Well, damn it, why don't you?"

"She's gone."

"So, it's not like we live in the Dark Ages. Go after her."

"What's the point?"

"What if she loves you?"

"I almost told her I loved her…back in Texas, but she made it very clear that she didn't love me. Very clear. I was hoping to change her mind. Apparently, I failed."

"The question is, why did she leave? I say she's unsure. You come back—this big rich guy. She's having problems. Hell, she wasn't expecting you. You married so quickly, she probably didn't know what to think. Here in London she was out of her element with your glitzy lifestyle and friends. Then the press made it worse by saying you and

Teresa should be together. You have to admit Teresa is beautiful. It would take a very confident woman to compete with a gorgeous countess, especially when some of your own friends seemed to think you preferred Teresa."

"But I don't. If I'd wanted Teresa, I would have married her."

"I know that, just as I know what you feel for Caitlyn and the boy. But does Caitlyn? What else have you two neglected to talk about? If this was a business deal, you wouldn't give up so easily. Go after her and get to the bottom of this. If not for your sake, for Daniel's. He needs to be part of a complete family. You and Caitlyn need to tell each other everything—the whole truth. You need to find out why she married Robert Wakefield. You need to tell her why you left her."

"She left me for Wakefield. That's why I left Texas."

"Have you discussed this with her? Once you've dealt with it openly and honestly, maybe then you can both forget."

"Until now, I preferred to forget about it without ever discussing it."

"Maybe she doesn't see it the same way. Communicating about what happens in our lives can be more important than the actual events."

"Maybe it's six years too late."

"Or maybe not. Forget your pride for once, before it costs you the thing you want most. Because of her, you've been a driven man for six years. What if neither of you can be as happy with other partners as you could be with each other? And then there's Daniel.... Put your pride aside and go to her—before it really is too late."

The shadows were long against a golden glaze of sunlight as Caitlyn stepped out of the house after dinner. Not that she noticed the beauty surrounding her.

She carelessly let the screen door bang behind her. Pulling a sweater over her shoulders against the chill, she headed across the pasture for a late-afternoon walk. The house was too lonely without Luke and Daniel.

Angel snorted a greeting as she trotted up behind her.

"Hey, big girl." Caitlyn pressed her cheek against Angel's neck for a long, consoling hug.

"Okay, no tears. I promise. But no carrots, either. We're just going for a walk."

Angel nodded as if she understood. After a little while, the two set off in silence.

Thirty minutes later, as they passed the oak motte on their way back to the house, the sunset streaked the darkening sky in incandescent pink and violet rays.

"Pretty night, isn't it, girl?"

Apparently Angel thought silence was the best answer, because she lowered her head and nibbled the high lush grasses.

Somewhere in the distance Caitlyn heard a whiny, whirring sound. Straining her ears, she tried to place it, but a breeze stirred through the trees and rattled the dry leaves, and she heard nothing more. Still, the sound made her think of Luke coming home every night in his helicopter.

A sharp pain pierced her. She missed him so much, especially at night. And because he was suddenly on her mind, she decided to venture inside the oak motte that held so many memories.

Silently, she walked through the trees until she came to the tree where Luke had carved their names. She'd lied to him when she'd told him their tree had been cut down. Placing her hand on the bark, she traced the rude letters, remembering too well how she'd stood behind him, watching breathlessly as he'd carved. Back then she'd thought he would love her forever.

"Luke," she whispered. "Oh, Luke.…"

Behind her, a boot crunched heavily on dry leaves.

She whirled as a tall, broad-shouldered man stepped out of the shadows. His long, easy gait was achingly familiar. So was his jet dark hair. Her heart raced. She couldn't believe what she was seeing.

"Luke? What are you doing here?"

"You told me our tree was gone."

"I wasn't entirely truthful."

"No. You weren't."

"What are you doing here?" she whispered.

"I'm here because I love you. Because I've always loved you. In the past. Now. Because I never stopped loving you."

"But you left me six years ago without even saying goodbye."

"Only because I thought you preferred Robert and didn't want me."

"I didn't prefer Robert! And I don't believe you ever thought I did! Why would you think that when I was always chasing after you? I was wild about you. Besides, I told you I had something important to tell you. I asked you to meet me here. But you didn't come."

"I got here early. Your mother was here waiting for me. Not you. She was standing right by this tree."

"My mother? How could she possibly have known to come here at that exact hour?"

"Apparently, she'd been watching us for some time. She said you were with Robert."

"Only because there had been an accident at his university. A college friend of his had died. She'd sent me over there earlier in the day to console him."

"Well, that's not what she told me. She said you were with him because you loved him, because you'd always loved him."

"But why would she lie?"

"She explained how his father had bought your ranch after the Wakefield bank foreclosed on you, how your marriage to Robert was the family's only chance to get the ranch back and make things right. She said I was standing in the way of all that, that he could give you everything and that I could give you nothing. She fired me on the spot and told me to take my things and clear out."

"She said you stole money, and she had to fire you."

"She told you that? I never stole anything in my life."

"She said you were worthless and worse than irresponsible to steal from a man who'd trusted you."

"If I'd done what she accused me of, she would have been right. I guess that's the only way she could be sure she'd be rid of me without your dad trying to track me down. She knew you and I made love in that barn. She said she watched us go in together, and she saw you later when you came out. She said it made her sick that you were wasting yourself on me. She told me if I stayed, I'd ruin your life, the same as my father ruined my mother's."

"Robert and I were good friends. Always. But nothing more."

"You married him."

"It's not like you think."

"I knew how much you loved your parents. I knew your mother was harder on you than your father was, way harder, but I believed that in time she'd convince you Robert was the right man for you. From that moment, I vowed to prove myself as good as any man. I became ruthlessly ambitious and I got richer beyond anything I'd ever imagined. But by then it was too late. I'd lost you."

"How could you leave without talking to me? Without calling to at least say goodbye?"

"I did call! And I wrote! I left messages."

"Well, I never got any of them. Not a single one."

"That's not what your mother told me. The last time I called she answered and ordered me to stop harassing you. She said that if you wanted to talk to me, you'd call. That you'd gotten all my messages and you had my number. I said, 'Put her on the phone.' She replied, 'She's married—to Robert Wakefield. Happily married.' Then she asked if I still wanted to talk to you. I slammed the phone down. I'll never forgive myself for not coming back, even then, to ask what you felt. All these years I thought you didn't love me, I was in hell."

A crushing pain for what he'd suffered and for what she'd suffered suffused her chest. Her dominating mother could have done everything he accused her of. She would have justified it, thinking it was the best thing for the family and the ranch.

Caitlyn sighed. "I was in a hell of my own, too. When I found out I was pregnant and you were gone, I didn't know what to do. That's why, in the end, I married Robert. I wanted Daniel to have a name."

"Not to get the ranch back?"

"That was part of it, but I thought mostly of Daniel. Of course, I knew the marriage made my mother and father happy. I won't lie about that. I liked pleasing them. In the end, since you were gone, I just saw it as the best solution for all concerned."

"I shouldn't have left without talking to you, without hearing your side. I should have come back. I will never forgive myself for abandoning you the way I did. You were right to hate me."

"Well, I forgive you," she said softly. "My mother could be very determined. Now that I know the truth, I feel betrayed…by her. I can't believe she made those decisions for me so high-handedly. And yet I can. She would definitely choose you now. She'd probably give herself total credit for you turning so well."

He laughed, but there was a bitter edge to his humor.

"I've been grieving for her so fiercely. This twist is going to take some getting used to. I can't help feeling very angry at her."

"She did what she did because she loved you."

"No, she saw me as a child, and she wanted to control me as one controls a child. She didn't know that I was grown, with a woman's heart. She had no idea the torture she put me through.

She misjudged you and Robert. His friend, the one who died...."

"What about him?"

"They were lovers. Robert was gay. His family didn't know. Nobody knew. Nobody except me. He'd come out to me when we were kids. When I told Robert I was pregnant, he told me about Joel. Robert married me because he couldn't imagine he'd ever love anybody else. But I think maybe he did. I think the marriage became an unendurable trap for him. I never told anybody until now... because in this county if you tell one person...."

Luke chuckled. "The whole county will know by dinnertime."

"And Teresa? What about Teresa?" she whispered.

"I love you."

"Why did you buy that house?"

"For you. For us. I bought it right after we got married. I couldn't see you running a horse farm in London, and I couldn't imagine you being happy for long without something more to do. Little boys need more space than my flat."

"What?"

"I know you'd rather live in Texas.…"

"One thing I've learned since coming back is that I want to be with you and Daniel, all of us together, more than anything…especially if I have my precious horses, too."

He kissed her. "I bought Mullsley Abbey for us, sweetheart. We can spend our vacations here at your beloved ranch, but when we're in the U.K., Mullsley Abbey is a short commute to London by helicopter or limo for me. We'll have plenty of room for more children. Out there, the pace of life is a bit slower, more like life here. We won't have to go to so many parties. And I intend to make some changes in my work schedule so we can have more time to be together. In short, it was to be a surprise wedding gift for you."

"And I thought…"

"The worst of me…as usual."

"Never again."

"Let us hope. But the tendency does run in the family. Your mother definitely saw only the worst in me. Occasionally, you have been known to do the same."

"Don't tease."

He laughed. Reaching for her hands, he pulled her closer.

"You really don't love Teresa?" she whispered.

"I love you. Only you." He wrapped her in his arms and held her tightly. "If you want the truth, I think she was mainly after my money."

Staring into his eyes, Caitlyn circled his neck with her arms, ran her fingers through his silky black hair. Then she framed his face with her hands. "I'm so glad you came back for me."

Bending down, he pressed his mouth to hers. "So am I."

He kissed her slowly as if to savor her taste and the silky texture of her lips. Warmth flooded her until she felt like she was overflowing with passion and happiness.

He loved her. He always had. Finally, she believed this miraculous truth.

Hand in hand they walked back to the house in the starlit darkness, Angel trailing them.

When they climbed the stairs to the porch, Luke pulled her into the shadows and kissed her again.

A chain squeaked noisily. "Does this mean I won't have to choose who to live with?" piped a treble voice from the swing at the end of the porch.

"Why, Daniel, honey!" she cried. "It's so good to see you! Where did you come from?"

"Daddy brought me. He told me to wait here at the house. Does this mean I can live with both of you? All the time?" he cried.

She went to him and touched his face just to make sure he was real.

"I'm sorry I went away." Threading her fingers through his dark bangs, she brushed them out of his eyes. "I missed you so much."

"But are you going to live with Daddy and me?"

"She sure is," Luke said, scooping him up into his arms.

"So, are we a real family now?" Daniel asked.

"You bet! I think this calls for a group hug just to prove it," Luke said.

"But no more kissing!" Daniel ordered sternly.

Luke made no promise. Curving his hand around Caitlyn's nape, he brought her close enough so he could whisper into her ear. "Later. We'll kiss later. We have the whole night.

"No, we have the rest of our lives."

Epilogue

Three years later

The rotor blades made a thunderous clap-clapping clamor as the helicopter whirred downward toward the lush, green countryside.

Luke loved coming home to Caitlyn and their children, but today, because of Caitlyn's news, his enthusiasm knew no bounds.

Another baby....

Lisa, their daughter, was two, so maybe it was time.

He leaned to one side and peered out of the helicopter. Usually he felt great pride when viewing Mullsley Abbey from the air. Up here he could see the ancient house in all its glory, its stately gardens, orchards, deer park and maze. But today his gaze was glued to the track where Caitlyn usually worked the horses she was training.

Strange. The track was empty. No sooner had the helicopter landed than he sprang out of it and ran toward the stables.

He thrust open a door and was about to enter the shadowy building when he heard her soft voice in the arena. Backtracking, he headed in that direction. All too soon he caught the pungent smell of sand flying from hooves.

Keeping to the shadows, so as not to interrupt the session, he watched her. Sasha, a temperamental stallion, had thrown back his head and was prancing sideways. Caitlyn was speaking to him calmly, waiting out his burst of temper. Finally, her stillness brought him to his senses, and they began to canter, moving like one.

She was magic on horseback. She was magic, period. The luckiest day of his life was the day he'd returned to Wild Horse Ranch.

All the pain of the past came screaming back through him, the years without Caitlyn and

Daniel, his anguish and the fury that had fueled his fierce ambition.

He didn't regret any of it.

For better or for worse....

He loved it all, the good and the bad. Loved her. Loved every minute of their lives together.

When Sasha whirled, and Caitlyn saw him, she gave a cry of pure joy that made the sun burn brighter and the trees sparkle with a fierceness that nearly blinded him. Quickly, she dismounted and handed the reins to a groom before turning and flying into his arms.

Wrapping her hands around his neck, she clung—just as she had when she'd been a girl and he'd kissed her for the first time.

He remembered everything, every moment they'd ever shared.

"Why didn't you tell me you were taking off early? I would have stopped working, showered.... Maybe even put on some lipstick."

"I wanted to surprise you. I like you just as you are."

She smiled, longing to believe him, but being female, she didn't quite.

He kissed her long and hard in a manner that left no doubt about the truth of his statement, or his intentions. "After you told me about the baby, I wanted to be with you. Only with you. I resented my business associates. If I'd stayed at the office, I would have abused everyone."

"Shame on you, darling."

"What do you say we make the most of my playing hooky?"

"What exactly do you have in mind?"

"I think you know, but just in case…" He whispered hot and provocative words into her ear that made her flush and laugh merrily. Then he grabbed her hand and tugged her in the direction of the stables.

"But not in…a stall," she said under her breath, giggling. "I'm afraid I really do have to draw a line…since someone might catch us."

"All right. If you refuse to indulge my darkest fantasies, inspired by our first time in the barn…"

Inside the tack room behind Sasha's stall, which smelled of leather and soap, he bolted the door and shoved her against the rough wall.

"Is this any way to treat a pregnant lady?" she teased as she began to unthread his tie. Using the silken ends, she reeled him closer.

"Just say the word, and I'll stop."

"Kiss me," she begged. "And then do all those wild, dirty things you just promised me you'd do."

Closing her eyes, she lifted her lips to his and abandoned herself to the wild exultation of their passion that fused not only their mouths and their bodies but their souls.

He stripped her slowly, garment by garment. When she was naked, he fell to his knees before her and paid homage with his lips and tongue to this woman he'd always adored.

"I love you," he murmured huskily afterward.

She closed her eyes and took a long, shuddering breath. "I love it when you say it like that."

For three years his joy in this woman had grown. No longer did he feel that some vital piece of himself was missing. With her by his side and in his bed, he was complete.

Tugging her close, he whispered against her ear,

"I love you. More than anything." Then he began to make love to her slowly as if they had all the time in the world. For once she didn't rush him.

* * * * *

Mills & Boon® Online

Discover more romance at
www.millsandboon.co.uk

 FREE online reads

 Books up to one
month before shops

 Browse our books
before you buy

...and much more!

For exclusive competitions and instant updates:

Like us on **facebook.com/romancehq**

Follow us on **twitter.com/millsandboonuk**

Join us on **community.millsandboon.co.uk**

Visit us Online | Sign up for our FREE eNewsletter at
www.millsandboon.co.uk